## "No need to run out like a scared virgin."

Mockery gleamed in Roarke's eyes. "Don't tell me my seminakedness upsets you?"

Joanna managed a shaky laugh. "Good grief," she answered, "do I look frightened?" She gave him what she hoped was a cool assessing look and then yawned daintily. "I'm tired, that's all. How's your head?"

"You'd better check," Roarke responded easily as he walked toward her.

Joanna wished she hadn't asked. "I, er..." she squeaked, her heart pounding. "It's healing nicely. Yes, so it is."

"I really do believe you're nervous, Miss Joanna," he mocked, enjoying the situation for some perverse reason of his own. "Very interesting!"

"Don't talk rubbish," she shot back. "I'm—I'm—" She froze in terror as his arms slid around her. "What are you doing?" she breathed.

# MARY WIBBERLEY

## law of the jungle

**Harlequin Books**

TORONTO • LONDON • LOS ANGELES • AMSTERDAM
SYDNEY • HAMBURG • PARIS • STOCKHOLM • ATHENS • TOKYO

Harlequin Presents first edition August 1982
ISBN 0-373-10526-6

Original hardcover edition published in 1982
by Mills & Boon Limited

# CHAPTER ONE

'It seems,' said the deep, cynical voice from behind Joanna's shoulder, 'as if you've just lost your escort.'

Joanna turned round very slowly. She was already bored and angry. Nobody, but *nobody*, ever abandoned her. Luis had done the unforgivable, and she didn't need this mocking comment from anyone. She opened her mouth, prepared to wither the man—and then she saw who it was.

She stared at him, her eyes cold with contempt. 'It seems as if *you've* lost your woman friend,' she said scathingly, 'as well. She obviously prefers Luis to you.'

'Ah. Is that his name?' The man seemed amused. 'So we're in the same boat—both abandoned. Shall we dance? Show them we don't care?' There was a disturbing edge of mockery in his deep voice.

She shrugged. Why not? she thought. She didn't care anyway. The party was too noisy, too drunken, too like all the others. She was getting bored with parties. Several couples had already vanished. They would reappear later—or then again they might not. That, too, was part of a familiar pattern.

It was cooler on the terrace, and no one else was there, just Joanna and the man. She had drunk too much champagne, and her silk stole slipped from her shoulders as he put his arms around her. He caught it and flung it over a nearby chair saying: 'You won't need that for a while.'

He held her lightly, not close. He was tall and big, very light on his feet. He was also dark, with shaggy black hair and a hard cynical face. He looked down at

5

her as they waltzed on the wide, empty, stone-flagged terrace. The fairy lights danced and gleamed overhead, caught in a slight breeze. 'Don't you mind?' Joanna enquired, looking up at him provocatively. A scene might relieve the tedium. She was getting bored with Luis as well anyway. His Latin charm had been wearing thin recently, and in another day Joanna was flying to Rio for the Mardi Gras carnival, and she didn't really care if she never saw Luis again...

'Mind? Bianca flirting with your boy-friend?' He appeared to ponder the question. 'Not particularly.'

'Perhaps you're wise,' she said sweetly. 'Luis *is* rather renowned for his quick temper——'

His laughter interrupted her. 'That doesn't bother me,' he answered.

'Really?' She smiled a small disbelieving smile that spoke volumes.

'No, really. I wouldn't fight over any woman.' His mouth twisted. 'Is that what you'd like?'

'I couldn't care less,' she snapped. 'Will you let me go now? I'm rather tired of dancing,' she hid a yawn.

He held her instead fractionally tighter. 'Or tired of parties?'

'Those too.'

'The night is young——'

'And so are we,' she finished. 'You don't need to start quoting. I've heard all the clichés before.'

'My name's Roarke,' he said, with an abrupt change of subject. 'What's yours?'

'Joanna,' she told him. 'Is that your first or second name?'

He shrugged. 'Does it matter?'

'Not to me,' she said flatly. 'Will you let me go now?'

'No. We're going to dance into the house through those french windows and I'll whisper sweet nothings in your ear and make sure that Luis sees us—and then we'll see what happens, shall we? He won't like it. Even if he himself is blatantly flirting with another woman he'll be sufficiently *macho* to resent you enjoying yourself with another man.'

'But you don't mind your Bianca——'

'I told you, as far as I'm concerned, no woman is worth fighting over.'

'Then why are you bothering?' she said. They had paused just outside the open terrace doors. Light spilled out, and music, and laughter. Everyone was having a good time.

'It might amuse *you*,' he said quietly. Joanna turned to look at him, and something made her shiver. It wasn't his expression, nor even the way he had spoken. It was something that went far deeper. He exuded a kind of quiet menace, as of controlled violence—as if he might erupt at any moment. She opened her mouth to speak, then closed it. Roarke was watching her. 'Scared?' he mocked.

'I'm not scared of anything,' she responded.

'I can believe that,' he said, but he was no longer looking at her, he was watching the woman he had brought talking to Luis in a nearby corner. The two stood, drinks in hands, eyes meeting, not touching each other—but they might well have been. Bianca's head was tilted slightly back, and her long dark hair cascaded over her shoulders. She wore a shimmering green dress, and she was a beautiful woman. Luis, tall and handsome, was clearly bowled over. They made a striking couple. Suddenly Joanna wanted to leave. She was not remotely in love with Luis, nor ever would be. She had met him at the house of friends in Manaos a week or so previously and he had been constantly at her side ever since, charming, attentive—and doing his best to get her to bed with him. Joanna had played a cool game, as she always had done, because she was used to having her way in any relationship as with everything else. She was rich, and she knew she was considered spoilt and selfish, and she didn't give a damn about anyone's opinion, because she had been brought up not to.

But something about the way they stood disturbed her. Some strong physical attraction was at work, and for a brief instant of time, she wondered . . .

'I don't want to go in,' she said. 'I'm going to leave.' She put up her hand to remove Roarke's from her arm, and he put his other hand over hers.

'I will, of course, take you home,' he said.

'I don't accept lifts from strangers,' she answered.

'Then how do you plan to travel?'

'Our hosts have a couple of chauffeurs, I believe——'

'It's three o'clock in the morning!'

'They're paid to drive.' She turned away from him, but he still held her. She took a deep breath. 'Will you let me go, or do you want me to cause a scene?'

'You would too, wouldn't you?'

'Yes, I would,' she answered calmly.

'Joanna Crozier, the girl who always gets her own way,' he said quietly. 'It'll be a change for Luis, meeting Bianca. She *likes* men.'

'Meaning I don't?' she snapped. 'And how did you know my name?'

'I recognised you. Who wouldn't? Your face is always in the newspapers. Your activities give the gossip columnists quite a bit of material, one way or the other. This must be a quiet holiday for you. There aren't so many in this part of Brazil.'

Joanna stood very still. 'So you knew who I was when you spoke to me before? It's a clumsy attempt at a pick-up, Mr Roarke—or whatever your name is.'

'When you told me your name, I remembered, and I wasn't attempting a pick-up—as you call it, merely sympathising with you in our mutual plight.' He shrugged. 'Still, I can't blame you for being suspicious. It must be hell for you, always wondering if it's you or your money a man is after.'

'You're exceedingly offensive!' she breathed, icily.

'Am I? And I wasn't even trying.' He laughed. 'And you're exceedingly prickly. Or are the personal comments only allowed to be one way?'

He took his hand from her arm as if he no longer wanted to touch her, and she turned to face him. She had never met a man like him before, and she found the fact quite illogically disturbing. He stood tall and big and powerful looking—and as if he felt sorry for her. That last fact was the one that disturbed. She couldn't care less, of course she couldn't, but no one ever reacted this way to a member of the Crozier clan. Joanna belonged to a family of winners, the best in everything they chose to be or do, and no one ever looked at a Crozier the way this man was looking at her. She wanted to tell him that, but instead she said something which surprised her even as she spoke.

'You may take me home,' she said.

He bowed. 'You're very kind,' he remarked. 'I am, of course, supposed to feel honoured?'

'You offered.'

'True,' he admitted. 'This way, then. We don't need to take our leave of our hosts, do we?'

'I don't imagine they'll notice.'

He touched her arm. 'Across the garden.' He pointed towards the dark trees. 'My helicopter is parked beyond there.'

That was certainly an original line. Joanna had travelled by helicopter many times, airport to airport, island hopping—but never from a party. She found the thought almost amusing. But she wouldn't give him the satisfaction of seeing her surprise, and said: 'Aren't you afraid of having it stolen?'

'No,' he said shortly, and handed her her stole and evening purse. 'I left somebody watching it.'

'At this time of night?'

'Yes. You're not the only one with money, you know.' It was a blunt answer, but effective. Joanna was momentarily silenced. They walked away from the house, towards the darkness, and when they touched the black night of the trees, Roarke said: 'Aren't you nervous? I am a stranger, after all.'

'No, I'm not. Should I be? I'm very capable of defending myself—or haven't you read all the gossip columns you profess to know so well?'

He laughed softly. '*Touché!* Yes, I'm well aware of your proficiency in karate. It would be a foolish man who tangled with you.'

'As long as we understand one another.' They were surrounded by darkness in the belt of trees. Joanna walked slightly ahead, feeling exhilarated in the strangest way. She didn't understand why, except that perhaps no one had touched her nerve ends like this man, made her feel alert to the barbed words that he spoke. Her boredom was with life, with everyone that she met, as rich, bland and bored as she, seeking excitement for its own sake, and then going on to more, because everything, after a time, palled.

'I'm not sure we do,' he responded. 'But it doesn't matter anyway. We're nearly there, then you can tell me where you're staying, and we'll take it from there.'

'I'm with friends about ten miles from here, outside Manaos, north—the Royos ranch.'

'Ah, I know it. Plenty of space for a helicopter to land. They're friends of yours?'

'Of my sister's.'

'I see. That's nice. You all visit each other, do you?'

'Do you really care, Mr Roarke?'

'No, I was trying to make polite conversation.'

They left the trees, and Joanna saw the helicopter waiting like a giant mosquito on the lawn, black and silent. 'I wouldn't have thought that came easily to you,' she said.

'It doesn't. How did you guess?' His deep voice, and everything that he said, scratched at her, claw-deep, mocking.

'You don't look like a man given to small talk. I'm surprised you went there tonight to the party.'

'I had some business to attend to.'

'And did you do it?'

'Yes.' He strode over to the door and opened it. Out of the corner of her eyes Joanna caught movement from nearby, a mere shadow that vanished, and she blinked, wondering if she had imagined it. 'In you get,' said Roarke, and took her and lifted her as though she were a child.

She felt a momentary qualm at his obvious strength. She was tall and slender, but no featherweight, yet Roarke had held her for a few seconds as though she were just that.

He sat beside her at the controls and she fastened her seat-belt and put on the headset that he indicated. She was silent as he fiddled with dials and knobs, sensing a professional, expert pilot. The lift-off justified her thoughts. It was smooth and practised, only the distant house and trees swiftly receding to tell her of their gaining height and speed.

His voice came into her ears. 'Comfortable?'

'Yes, thank you.'

'Good. Just relax, we're on our way.'

There was no more conversation. Not for fifteen or so minutes when Joanna felt the first faint twinges of uneasiness. 'Roarke,' she asked, 'when will we be there?'

'Soon.'

She looked out. The lights of Manaos had disappeared. All was blackness outside, with no landmarks to tell her where they were. She estimated their speed as between thirty and forty miles an hour, and at that rate they should have been near to the Royos ranch, yet he wasn't losing height as he ought to have been. They were maintaining both speed and height, if anything, fractionally increasing both.

'Do you know where we are?' she asked, after another minute had elapsed.

'Yes, I do. Relax.'

'But we should be nearly——'

'I'm the pilot, Joanna.' His voice had changed. She couldn't have said in what way, but this wasn't the man who had danced with her on the terrace at a party. Something caught in her throat—not fear exactly, more puzzlement. There was a hard, clipped incisiveness to his words. There was something almost menacing about them.

'I know you are,' she answered calmly. 'But I think you're going in the wrong direction.'

'It all depends where you think we're going.'

Distorted by the headphones, his voice had a flat, metallic ring to it that only made the words more unreal. And they were unreal enough in themselves.

'We're going to my friend's ranch.'

'No, I'm afraid we're not.'

She knew then, when it was too late, that she should never have come. But it *was* too late, and whatever was happening, wishful thinking would not make it otherwise.

'I see,' she said calmly. 'Are you kidnapping me?'

'No. And I'm not going to harm you. Whether you believe it or not, that's the truth. You will not be harmed in any way. But I am taking you somewhere, and we'll be in the air for another forty minutes. There's nothing that you can say or do that will make me alter course, so you may save your breath. And if you attempt any physical activity I'll stop you. I'm piloting this helicopter and I won't allow you to do anything that will put us in danger. Do I make myself clear?'

She breathed deeply. 'No, you don't. Why won't you tell me where we're going, and why?'

'Because it wouldn't mean anything to you. I'm taking you somewhere you won't recognise. You'll be safe there. And I'm not at liberty to tell you why.'

'The only reason is money,' Joanna said flatly and very clearly.

'There you're mistaken. Money might be the only reason *you* can ever think of for anything, but it's not mine. You're not going to be held for ransom. You'll just have to take my word on that.'

'Your word? Am I supposed to be impressed? My God!'

'If you want a drink there's a flask beside you. It has orange juice in. Any insults you care to hurl won't affect me.'

She looked at him. In the eerie bluish light from the controls his face was almost frightening. She had seen him only dimly before. They hadn't gone in among the strong bright lights of the house. She didn't know anything about him except his name, Roarke, and even that was probably false. She sat back and consciously tried to calm her mind, so as to clear it. The shock had already sobered her and her brain was sharp and keen, the adrenalin flowing. Her one thought now was escape. Any alternative was intolerable. She had piloted a helicopter herself on occasion, and she studied his hands now at the controls, and took in all the information she could glean, watching, noting, taking her time. Then she mentally went over the contents of her evening bag. Comb, purse, lipstick, handkerchief, perfume. The perfume was in a spray, the comb of metal. Both could serve as weapons. Her evening sandals, although flimsy, had high stiletto heels. She practised slipping her feet in and out so as to have them ready for use when the moment arose. She clasped her hands on her knees, flexing and exercising her fingers so that they would be supple when needed. She breathed deeply, counting and holding, special exercises to prepare body and mind mentally for supreme effort when the time came.

Joanna was spoilt and wilful. She was also, like all the other members of her family, superbly fit and healthy. Few people had ever got the better of a Crozier, and this man, whoever he was, she had already decided was not going to get the better of her. He was in for quite a shock!

They were coming in to land. Neither had spoken for what seemed ages, but for Joanna the time had been filled with inner, secret activity. Apparently docile and resigned to her fate, inside she was charged with explosive energy.

Lower and lower they went, and Roarke spoke. 'Hold on tight.'

She obeyed, but she didn't answer. It was better that she protested when he helped her out, or he might be suspicious. Better still if she put on a show of sheer temper. A gentle bump, and the engines faltered and died, the rotor blades click-clicking to a halt.

She unfastened her seat-belt and said in a voice filled with trembling fury: 'Would you mind telling me what the hell's going on?'

'Let's get out first, shall we?'

She followed him, crouching slightly, and he jumped down and waited for her, holding up his hands for her to follow. She stood instead in the doorway and shouted: 'No, damn you! I want to know what you're up to before I leave this——' But hidden behind her apparent temper was the calm brain, now ready for action. And this could be the ideal moment. He was vulnerable, two or three feet below, waiting.

'I'll tell. Jump—it's not far.' She jumped, barefooted, having removed her sandals silently moments before, and kicked out with deadly accuracy for his throat. He should have gone flying, knocked unconscious. He should have, but he didn't, because he moved as swiftly as Joanna, or even swifter, she could never be sure of that, and suddenly the world turned upside down, and she was lying on the ground helpless, and he was holding her. She couldn't move. Glaring up at him, she breathed hard, fighting for control after his lightning counter-move.

'No, Joanna,' he said softly, 'it won't work. Get up. You tried, but I'm better than you.' And he pulled her to her feet. She faced him, and she knew then. 'You didn't think I was that stupid, did you?' he grated. 'I wanted to see if you'd try anything. Go back and get your sandals now.'

She stared at him. 'No, I won't!' she spat.

'Then you'll walk barefoot.' He didn't seem to care either way. He took hold of her hand and began walking away. The ground was rough and she stumbled and wrenched her arm free and caught him a stinging blow on his head. He took her, picked her up and carried her, struggling vainly in a grip of steel, towards the large house nearby.

It was surrounded by trees, and a light gleamed in the hall lighting their path to it, showing steps, a high arched doorway, and a door standing wide open. He walked up the steps with her and put her down in the hall, and she looked around her, stunned with disbelief.

It was like entering a fairy castle. Nothing had prepared her for this. The light from a chandelier in the centre of the ceiling showed the gracious stairway curving upwards into shadows, and lit the deep red carpet on the floor. Antique chairs and cupboard stood, polished and beautiful, gleaming with love and care, and there was even an Adam fireplace with an oil painting of a woman above the mantelpiece. Joanna, silent now, looked around her and didn't believe what she was seeing. It was like walking into an English country mansion. Yet she was in Brazil, in Amazonia. Unless she was dreaming, and, after all that had happened, she was beginning to wonder.

'Where are we?' she asked at last.

'In the middle of nowhere.'

She turned towards the waiting man who had told her his name was Roarke and faced him with head held high, seeing him properly for the first time. And, for the first time, she was afraid.

# CHAPTER TWO

ROARKE stood tall and easy, just watching her, apparently relaxed, yet as deadly as a jungle animal waiting to pounce. The normal person would not have been aware of it; only Joanna, mind super-tuned to the danger she was in, could sense it. She had met her match, and she didn't like it. She noticed too the things she hadn't noticed before—the suit he was wearing, that she had taken for denim jeans and jacket, faded and well worn, had, in the light, the unmistakable stamp of superb cut and quality. His jacket was unbuttoned, revealing a hard hairy chest, as tanned as his face and hands. A strong face, his eyes dark and narrowed as he, in his turn, watched her. He had a wide mouth—sensual or cruel, hard to tell; it could be both. His chin was stubborn, with a cleft in it, his nose large, his cheekbones high, lending his face a Slavic air. None of these things had Joanna seen before. He had just been a man who spoke barbed words, and she had met plenty of those before, and knew how to deal with them.

Now he smiled. There was nothing gentle about it, it didn't soften his features, but he was amused. 'Seen all you want to?'

'I'm just looking to see what kind of man it is who can abduct a woman.'

'Look away.' He held his hands out, palms up. 'There's no charge. Am I supposed to feel flattered?'

She didn't answer. She turned away, no longer wanting to watch his expression, and went and opened one of the doors leading off from the hall.

It was in darkness and she felt for the switch and

light flooded the room. It was a drawing room, all pale
gold and creams, and exquisitely furnished, cool, ele-
gant. Pictures covered the pale cream walls and plants
abounded on every surface. She walked in, looked
around, and Roarke silently followed.

'Nice place,' he remarked.

'Is it yours?'

'No. Time for bed. I'll show you your room.'

She turned to face him. 'I'm not going anywhere until
I know what we're doing here.'

'Then you'll stand here a long time, Joanna, because
I'm not going to tell you. Let's just say you're a house
guest for the time being. And before you even think of
it, let me also tell you, we're completely surrounded by
jungle—which, I don't need to remind you, is full of
deadly danger. Escape is quite out of the question. Even
if you knew where we were, which you don't, you
wouldn't get more than a few yards. I've immobilised
the helicopter, so there's no use you trying to fly it. I
saw you watching me at the controls, and I wouldn't
put it past you to try. The house is quite safe, and once
I've locked the door, no one can get either in or out.
Have I made myself clear?'

'I'm a prisoner.'

'A dramatic way of putting it, but, for the moment,
yes. Now, I'm tired. I've had a busy day and I'm going
to bed.' And he turned and walked out. Joanna heard
bolts being pulled home, a key turning. Quickly she
darted to the nearest window and tried to open it. It
refused to budge. She was still there when Roarke
returned.

'Are we alone in the house?' she demanded.

'There are two servants, an Indian couple, neither of
whom speak English, nor hardly any Portuguese. They
speak a kind of patois, an Indian dialect. And there are
the birds.'

'Birds?' she repeated. 'What kind?'

He shrugged. 'You'll see later. It's nearly five in the morning. Aren't you tired?'

'How the hell do you expect me to sleep?' She walked towards him and stood before him, defiance in every inch of her—yet a slightly wary defiance. She had twice now experienced his strength, and she had sufficient respect for it not to try anything again—yet. He wouldn't always be as wide awake as he appeared now. Even the strongest man had to sleep some time.

'I don't really care. Do you want any food or drink before we go up?'

'No, I don't. And what are the sleeping arrangements?'

'They don't include me, if that's what's in your mind. You have a room and bathroom to yourself——'

'How kind!' she cut in scathingly.

'It must make a change for you anyway,' he shot back.

'And *what* precisely do you mean by that?'

The corner of his mouth twitched. 'Think about it. You'll have plenty of time to do that over the next day or two. You might also reflect on your life style while you're about it.'

Joanna went very still. Eyes blazing into his, she demanded in a low furious voice: 'Tell me what 'you mean.'

'You need to ask? You, Joanna Crozier, playgirl of the Western World——' he got no further. Incensed, she lashed out and struck him hard, a stinging, satisfying blow across his face that wiped the smile from it. Breathing hard, no longer caring what he did in retaliation, she remained where she was—and he laughed. He actually laughed.

'Was that supposed to hurt? It would take more than——'

'Then how do you——' but her arm never reached its target the second time. He caught her wrist, held it, and slowly, easily, pulled her towards him.

'It doesn't give you licence to repeat the action,' he said softly, and she winced at the subtle pressure on her wrist. He could break it if he chose, they both knew it. His dark grey eyes mocked her, as did he. She thought she had never met anyone she so loathed. Defiantly, hiding the pain, she glared at him. For a few moments they were both still, the silent messages of the eyes saying more than words could. It was all there. Then he released her. She didn't rub her wrist; she wouldn't give him that satisfaction. She put her hand to her side. The wrist throbbed and ached.

'You are contemptible,' she said.

'Am I? That's your opinion. You might have cause to change it. Are you walking upstairs or do I have to carry you?'

'I'll walk. I might be sick if you touched me!'

She went towards the door and he followed, switching out the light after them. Roarke led her to a wide landing at the top of the stairs and opened a door to his right. The light came on and she saw an elegantly furnished bedroom, with fitted wardrobes and dressing table in a light wood, polished wooden floor with scatter rugs in bright colours, and a large bed covered with a gold-coloured bedspread; the overall effect was of cool comfort.

He opened drawers in a chest. 'Night clothes and underwear,' he told her, 'and in the wardrobe,' he opened the sliding door, 'all the clothes you'll need for a few days.'

Joanna knew, finally. She had begun to guess on the journey, but this confirmed it. She closed the bedroom door behind her. 'How long has this been planned?' she asked. She was determined to get some answers at least before he left. A cold, deadly anger filled her that overcame all her previous fear.

He slid the wardrobe door shut. 'About a week.'

'And the—incident—at the party. Was that also planned?'

'Luis being seduced by my girl-friend? Yes.'

'Was that the business you had to attend to?'

'The business was you, Joanna.'

'And if I'd refused to let you take me home?'

He shrugged. 'Then, or later, you would have come with me. I'm like you in that respect. If I set out to do something, I do it. Failure is not a word in my vocabulary.' His voice held no conceit or arrogance, as it might have done. It was matter-of-fact, and that was more chilling. It made her feel helpless, and she had never felt helpless in her life.

'Dear God,' as she whispered the words, all anger drained away. Suddenly she was so tired; it swept over her in a wave, and she swayed slightly, ashamed of her weakness, yet unable to do anything about it. Roarke looked at her. There was no softening on his face, for which she was, in a way, grateful. She needed no one's pity, not her. 'Get out,' she said.

He walked towards the door, opened it, turned, looked at her, then went out. Joanna heard a lock click after he had closed the door and she went over to the bed and sat down, legs rubbery. For a few minutes she sat without moving. A dry ache was in her throat, and her head throbbed. She felt lost, alone, utterly bewildered. For the first time in her life she didn't know what to do. She put her hands to her face and wept.

When Joanna awoke, the sun streamed in through the closed windows, yet the room was cool. The air-conditioning was silent and efficient, for the air was fresh and sweet. She slid out of bed feeling wretched, and went to her bathroom for a long, cool shower. Everything she could need was there, in a cupboard—two new toothbrushes, toothpaste, deodorant, talc and toilet water. There was even a jar of moisture cream, and it was the brand she always used. It was almost as though her every taste was known, another disturbing fact.

She knew even before she looked that the clothes would fit her. They too were brand new; three cotton sundresses, three skirts in brightly patterned cotton, and several tops. They were not quite to her taste, but they were light and attractive. There was also a pair of flat leather sandals in her exact size. The underwear in the drawers, several pairs of pants, bras, and nighties, was also correct. It was like a waking nightmare—but it was not yet finished. There was something else, which she found as she systematically searched the room. In the drawer of her bedside cupboard was a large brown envelope which she opened. A pile of photographs fell on to the bed, slithering and shiny. She picked them up. They were all of her—but she wasn't aware of them having been taken at any time. One of them, with an instantly recognisable background, had been taken on a recent holiday in Monte Carlo. She was on the deck of a yacht with several friends. The print was very clear. She had been wearing a bikini, and was very tanned, as were all the others aboard. One of the men had just opened a bottle of champagne and it had showered over them all, having been shaken first, and they were all shrieking with laughter. The camera had caught and frozen that moment in time for ever. It had been a breakfast celebration following an all-night party aboard the boat which had finished only an hour or so previously. She put that photograph down and looked at the next, and her heart gave a little bump. Two men were fighting in the background; and Joanna was standing with another girl watching them, and laughing. It had been good fun at the time, she remembered that, because the fight had been over her. Only now, looking at it, it didn't seem so funny. She had not been aware of anyone taking a photograph. The other girl, some model from London that Joanna knew slightly, had been clutching Joanna's arm, and they were laughing, laughing for ever into a film that she was now looking at. Both the men had been drunk, and the scrap had ended in confusion, and bloodied noses and then champagne, and all forgotten. She couldn't even remember exactly what the fight had been about, now. She put the pictures down, not wishing to see any more, and went to the door. It opened at a touch.

She dressed and went down the stairs. The front door, when she tried it, opened silently, much to her surprise. She walked down the steps and saw the helicopter a distance away. Beyond it, the thick impenetrable jungle. Silently, Joanna walked round the house. It was very large, with tall windows, some of them shuttered. The air was intensely hot and humid and she was perspiring freely after only a few yards. The jungle noises, never far away, were a constant reminder of her vulnerability; the chatter of monkeys, the shriek of birds, shrill animal cries, whoops and yells. Hollow sounds, eerie and disturbing. Even more disturbing was the fact that she had no idea where she was. Still on Brazilian soil, undoubtedly, but that was no help. She brushed her short blonde hair away from her face. She had the feeling of being watched, which was in a way as unsettling as the photographs had been. It was almost with a sense of relief that she rounded the last corner and reached the front of the house again.

Roarke was waiting for her. He was dressed entirely in black—black open shirt, tight black trousers, black thonged sandals. He watched her approach, and to Joanna's already over-sensitive imagination, looked faintly sinister. The black clothes helped the image, of course. He looked all-powerful, impatient, controlled violence ready to be unleashed.

'Had a good look round?' he asked.

'Yes. You obviously expected me to, or you wouldn't have unlocked the doors.'

'Of course.' He followed her up the steps and closed the front door. The cool air inside the house was balm to her skin, and she took a deep breath.

'This way. Breakfast is ready.' He led her into another room which led off the main entrance hall. The long dining table was set for two, and a woman appeared silently and watched Joanna unblinkingly with button black eyes. She was small, with flat Indian features and an impassive expression. Roarke said something to her and she nodded and disappeared again. At least he had spoken the truth in something. They were not entirely alone.

'Sit down, Joanna,' he said, and she did so. A bowl of fruit was on the table, bananas, oranges, mangoes and limes. The woman reappeared carrying two plates which she put in front of them, muttering something as she did so. She went out, to return a moment later with a plate of crusty black bread and a bowl of butter.

Joanna looked in dismay at what was on her plate. It looked like tiny pieces of white fish in thin sauce. But she was hungry, much to her surprise, and began to eat. The fish was delicately flavoured and quite delicious. Roarke poured out two glasses of orange juice from a jug that clinked with ice, and Joanna drank thirstily.

'The water in your taps is quite safe to drink,' he remarked. 'It's specially filtered and treated. It might not taste as good as you'd like, but you won't be ill.'

'How kind,' she murmured. 'It's nice to know you're so concerned for my welfare,' and she looked at him.

'You'll learn,' he answered, equally quietly. 'Insults don't bother me, so you may say what you like. But you might as well save your breath for other things.'

'Such as what?' she demanded.

'Such as thinking.'

'You said that last night. Is that why the photos were in my bedroom? To make me think?'

'Ah, you found them.'

'Yes. Did you take them?'

He looked faintly surprised. 'Me? No, I've better things to do.'

'Like abducting women from parties? I suppose that's a matter of opinion. Personally, I'd think a sewer worker could take more pride in what he does than you.' She broke a piece of the crusty bread in two, and buttered it.

'You were brought here to meet someone.'

His words took her by surprise. She hadn't expected to be told anything, and she stared at him. 'What did you say?'

His eyes met hers. 'I said you were brought here to meet someone.'

'Who?'

'You'll find out when he arrives.'

He? It was a man. But whom? 'You mean all this elaborate charade—the scene at the party, the helicopter journey, the clothes ready—all those are because someone is coming here to meet me? You must be mad to expect me to believe that,' she answered.

'I'm not mad, nor is he. And before you ask, it was the only way to do it.'

'Did "he" take the photographs?'

'I doubt it very much.'

'Is this his house?'

'Yes, of course. And I'll show you round it after we've eaten.'

'Please tell me who it is,' she said quietly, and he looked at her, amused.

'Please? That's a new word for you, isn't it? I'm sorry, I can't. One, because I gave him my word, and two, because you wouldn't believe me if I did.'

'I'll pay you well.'

His expression changed. 'I don't get bought by anyone.'

'He hired you, didn't he?'

'Not exactly.' He gave her a hard, level glance. 'Is that how you regard people? As marketable commodities? Money buys anything—or anyone? You'll find out how wrong you are when you meet him.'

'And when will that be?'

'Very soon. Tomorrow I hope.'

'If this is his house, why isn't he already here?' she asked.

'Because he travels a lot. He's been in Europe recently, and he wasn't able to get here before now—but your holiday in Manaos provided the ideal opportunity, and I took it.'

'Have you been following me around?' Joanna demanded.

'No, I haven't. Someone else has, though.'

'Who?'

'A private detective.'

'My God! I'm not a criminal!' she exclaimed.

'I never said you were. You asked—I told you. Private detectives don't usually follow criminals about anyway, they leave that to the police if they've any sense.'

'Then why? *Why?*'

Roarke stood up. 'I've told you enough. You've finished eating. We'll go.'

She remained seated. 'I don't want to go anywhere. I don't want to see the house. I want to stay here.'

'Very well.' He sat down again. 'But I'll not tell you more.'

Joanna glanced at him. He produced a box, took out

a cheroot from it, and then a lighter from his pocket. 'Want one?' he asked.

'No, thanks.'

'Don't you smoke?'

'No. Should I?'

He shrugged. 'Moving in your crowd, I would have thought so. What is it with you, then? Drugs?'

'No. Do I look as though I take drugs?'

'No. You look healthy.' He lit the cheroot and surveyed her through a thin wreath of blue smoke. 'Which surprised me when I met you.'

An idea was forming in Joanna's mind. There was more than one way of finding out things she wanted to know, and she was prepared to use stronger tactics. She relaxed slightly, and smiled at him. Not a big smile, nothing to give him cause for wariness, but a slight, almost resigned one.

'Because of the crowd I mix with,' she said wryly. 'You've seen the photos?'

'Yes, I have.'

'A lot of them do take drugs—I imagine you know that. But I've more respect for my body. I've seen what they can do.'

'Yet you run around with the fast set, living it up, partying, yachting in the Mediterranean——'

'What else is there to do when you're a bored little rich girl?' she asked, and batted her eyelashes at him. If this was a game she could play it as well as he, and alter the rules if it suited her. She had his measure now. Tough, hard as nails and powerful—but still a man. She would needle him first, provoke him to anger, and wait her moment.

She saw the imperceptible tightening of his mouth, a muscle moving in his cheek, and felt a slight edge of triumph. She lowered her head slightly and then put her hand to her chin, fingers resting lightly on it, and looked upward at him in a faintly submissive manner. 'It's not my fault if I'm rich. I live in a different world from most people. I'm sorry if that offends you, Roarke, but there it is. And whoever took those candid camera shots was watching me carefully—although I wasn't aware of it. I don't intend to apologise for my way of life, because I don't know any other.'

'And you like it?'

She chuckled throatily. 'I wouldn't change it for anything!'

'That wasn't the impression I got last night at the party.'

'Oh, *that*,' she pulled a face, a pretty little pout. 'I was annoyed with Luis, that was all—and the party was boring.' Then she suddenly remembered something. 'The people I'm staying with——'

'They've been told you've gone to visit friends you met unexpectedly. They're quite satisfied.'

'Ah. Your lady-friend Bianca?'

'Yes, that was arranged too.'

'All well thought out, in fact,' she laughed. Her inner feelings wouldn't show any more. Let him think that she was resigned—albeit reluctantly—to her fate. But she wasn't. Her head was very cool and clear. 'Tell me, is Bianca your mistress? She's very beautiful.'

'She is, isn't she? No, she's not. She's the wife of a very good friend of mine, and I don't poach on other men's preserves. She was merely a decoy to lure Luis away.'

'Hmm,' she said. 'I saw the way she was looking at him. The atmosphere was pretty electric.'

'You noticed that too? She's an actress—and a very good one.' He put down his cheroot. 'You don't miss much, do you?'

'I wasn't supposed to, was I?'

'No. That was the purpose of the exercise.'

'And it worked,' she said softly. 'I'm here, and that's precisely what you wanted. Do you feel pleased?'

He regarded her evenly. 'Neither pleased nor displeased. I have other work to do as soon as I leave here.'

'And are you going to tell me—or is that on the list of things you're not going to talk about?'

'I can tell you a little. I organise expeditions to remote areas of South America. Not only Brazil, but Colombia, Peru, Paraguay, Argentina—most everywhere in this vast continent—for people who want to find lost cities, search for emeralds, discover Inca gold—or just explore untouched areas of savage beauty that few have ever seen before.' He paused. Joanna, despite herself, was fascinated. She was going to have pretended an interest in whatever he did, as part of her plan—but the reality of it took her breath away.

Roarke was watching her. 'It sounds wonderful,' she said, and those were the first completely sincere words she had said to him. 'Is it ever dangerous?'

He laughed. 'Not if I can help it—but yes, there have been one or two hairy moments.'

Joanna felt a little frisson of fear mingled with excitement. Looking at him, at that controlled exterior, she could imagine how he would react in a tight corner, and the image was faintly disturbing, because no one she had ever known had been like this man. She didn't—couldn't—ever like him, because of what he had done to her, but she could respect a man who was so very powerful. She had heard it said that power was an aphrodisiac, that men of great power in world affairs were sought out by women wherever they went. For the first time in her life she understood it fully. Like him or loathe him, there was something incredibly attractive about him. It threw her momentarily from her chosen course.

'That explains your skill in karate,' she said, recovering fast, keeping her tone dry.

'It's been useful, on occasions. I was a marine commando for six years as well. What I learned there has also helped, on occasions.' He smiled slightly, reminiscently. It was like seeing another world open up, another kind of life, alien to Joanna—beyond her understanding, yet obviously as real as her own world. Perhaps more real after all. Roarke would be a formidable adversary. And that was what they were. The glimpse of another world, another place, vanished. His life was not hers. He had no right to do what he had done. He was the enemy. He would be even more of a challenge, that was all. She felt a tingle in her blood, a quickening of her pulses, and she smiled, her eyes warmer as she looked at him.

'Thanks for the warning,' she murmured. 'I won't try and escape again.' She rose gracefully to her feet, smoothing down her dress in an apparently casual movement. 'Will you show me round now?'

He stubbed out his cheroot and followed her to the door. She didn't see the expression on his face. She might not have felt so confident if she had.

He saved the aviary until the last. It was at the back of the house, a huge airy room that had obviously been two at one time. It had an inner door of fine mesh. Joanna gasped when she went in, and stood for a moment outside the mesh partition. 'Are you nervous of birds?' Roarke asked, and she shook her head. He had to shout, for the noise was indescribable, shrieks of macaws and parrots drowning out the quieter chirrupings of the smaller exotically plumaged birds that flew and swooped and fluttered among the lush green jungle in miniature of the aviary. He locked the outer door and opened the inner mesh so that they could go in. It was like being in a forest, surrounded by foliage, the air damp and humid in great contrast to the air-conditioned coolness of the rest of the house. There was a path of sorts, and a bench in the centre of the enormous place. A vividly coloured parakeet glared at them, squawked harshly as it rose from the bench, and flew on to Roarke's shoulder. Joanna repressed a smile as she sat down, followed rather gingerly a moment later by him. 'They're all fairly tame,' he said loudly, above the din, and the bird mocked his voice. 'Tame, tame, tame,' it shrieked.

He winced. 'And noisy,' he added.

There were troughs of water, and longer troughs containing what looked like nuts and seeds. A tiny bright azure blue bird stopped to sip from a drinking tube suspended on a branch before darting away, and Joanna looked round her in frank wonderment. The man who owned the house, who planned to meet her, obviously loved birds. The room was big enough for all to fly freely, protected from natural predators, and the plants had been well chosen to provide natural nourishment. It was a safe world for them.

Roarke touched her arm. 'Seen enough?' he mouthed, and she nodded. The parakeet was trying to peck his top button. There was a sudden loud crunch, and it fell to the ground in two pieces. Joanna bent and picked the broken button up and they walked towards the entrance. The bird flew away, uttering something that sounded suspiciously like a scornful laugh, and then they were outside the mesh. A feather fluttered from Joanna's hair, and she shook her head as Roarke opened the outer door.

'Need a drink?' he asked.

'Yes. Something cool, please.'

He led the way down, into the hall, then the drawing room. 'I'll not be a minute,' he told her. 'Make yourself comfortable.' She waited until he had gone and then went over to the long wall mirror. Opening her evening bag—the only one she had with her—she found comb and lipstick, and used them. Her face looked back at her, warm, glowing, reassuringly attractive. Deep blue eyes, darkly lashed, fine clear brows. She frowned, damped her finger, and smoothed them neatly. It was a nuisance having no make-up, but nature had been generous and she needed little. Her eyes sparkled with the light of battle, and her soft full mouth curved in a little smile. She'd do. She had never had to assess herself like this before—but then it had never been necessary. She had never been in a conflict like this. She did not intend to stay tamely, her life under another's control. No Crozier would ever allow it, and Joanna was a true Crozier—and tough. Not as tough as Roarke, but then who could be? Her weapons were of a different kind, and possibly more powerful. Time would tell, and it wasn't on her side. She had today, that was all. She pulled a face at her dress. It was simple, not at all what she would have chosen for herself. Never mind, it would have to do——

The door opened and Roarke came in with a tray holding two glasses and a jug. He put them down on a small coffee table by the fireplace.

'Why the fireplace?' she asked. 'In the jungle?'

'Only for decoration. A touch of England.'

'So he's English?'

'Yes,' he answered, and handed her a filled glass. She sipped. It was orange juice—and something else.

'Vodka?' she asked.

'Yes, but not a lot.'

'Very civilised.' She drank more. 'I shall need a siesta after lunch.'

'You may have it, of course.'

'And will you?'

'I might. We didn't get much sleep last night, did we?'

'Not a lot.' She yawned at the reminder. 'Oh dear, excuse me. When's lunch?'

'When do you want it?'

'To be honest, I don't. I'm not hungry.'

'Then we'll eat later.' He put down his glass. 'I'll tell Sanara.' He went out. Joanna didn't know exactly what she was going to do, but her mind was busy. She was taking a gamble and the stakes were high, but so was the prize, freedom. That was more important than anything else. She poured herself another drink and waited for Roarke to return.

# CHAPTER THREE

JOANNA studied the photographs again after she went to her room, seeking a clue as to who might have taken them, or wanted them taken. That was more important. Who was this man who had gone to such elaborate lengths to get her into his house? And for what reason? That was the question that had been in her mind ever since Roarke had brought her. She could think of no one. An ex-boy-friend, secret admirer? Enemy? All were possible, but hardly probable. Yet it was very disturbing not to know. It all came back to money as far as she was concerned, she decided. There might even be a ransom demand out for her now, despite Roarke's denials—and certainly no one would ever find her here. She had no idea herself where she was. They would send the message to her mother.

Joanna thought about that for a moment, thought about her mother. Margot Crozier, glittering socialite on the New York and London scene, daughter of Errol Crozier, the man who had made millions with his stores that graced the best streets of every large city in Europe and the United States, was a woman whose life was bound up totally in herself. Everything revolved around her, and at forty-seven she was a stunning-looking red-head whose love life was a constant source of joy to the gossip columnists of the world. She had resumed her maiden name when her husband, Joanna's father, had died. Joanna had never known her father, for she had only been a few months old when he was lost at sea, and her sister Laura had been not much older. Her mother had afterwards never spoken about him,

something Joanna had felt keenly when young, especially at end of term in school, when her friends had been
met by their parents. There had been 'uncles', of course.
Her mother had never been without admirers, or 'good
friends' as the newspapers would gleefully put it.

Joanna wondered how her mother would react. She
had last seen her a month previously in London, and
then only for a brief time, lunch at the Ritz, coffee
afterwards, a kiss on the cheek, and a farewell. Margot
didn't like being reminded that she was the mother of
two young women in their twenties. She wouldn't react
in the typical motherly way when—and if—a ransom
note was received. No hysterics, panic or shock. More
likely anger at the stupidity of Joanna for getting herself
abducted.

'Oh, Mother,' she said softly now, 'if only you knew!'
But she didn't know why she had said it. A sudden,
empty feeling filled her, a hollow, aching pain, and she
didn't understand that either.

Her grandfather, Errol Crozier, had died three years
previously and his huge fortune had gone to his sons
and daughters and grandchildren. Joanna was wealthy
in her own right, as were her sister and many cousins.
She had always got on well with her grandfather, and it
had been a shock, after he died, to read the newspaper
obituaries. 'Ruthless egomaniac,' one of the milder de-
scriptions, had distressed her. He had been kind enough,
although remote, to Joanna and Laura. She had refused
to read any more after that. People, certainly not newspapers, didn't understand. Her mother had dismissed
all reports with the acid comment that everyone was
jealous of those with money. Joanna accepted this. It
was quite logical, and she had gone on her merry way,
and life had become even more hectic in the frantic
search for pleasure.

Now, sitting on her bed, photographs in hand, she

began to wonder; where was it all leading? She looked around the room. To here, apparently, for an appointment with someone unknown. She was no nearer guessing whom. Roarke was her only link. He knew. He knew everything—and he was telling nothing.

She flung the pictures down, stood up and went to her door and opened it. The house, save for distant bird noises, was quiet. She went to Roarke's door and tapped on it. There was no answer. She waited a moment, then cautiously tried the handle. The door opened and she went into see him lying on the bed clad only in the black trousers, flat on his back. He opened his eyes as she entered.

'Come in,' he said drily. She already was. She went over to the bed and sat down on it and looked at him.

'Tell me—please,' she said.

'Tell you what?' He lay there unmoving and unmoved, perfectly relaxed. He had drawn his blinds, and the room was dim and shadowy. 'Do you think it wise to enter a man's bedroom when he's in bed?'

Joanna gave a faint smile. 'I don't think you're going to try and rape me, are you?'

'No. The thought had never crossed my mind. It's obviously crossed yours though.'

'Not unnaturally,' she agreed. 'It has been known for kidnappers——'

'Which I am not.'

'So you say. How do I know my mother's not opening a ransom note at this moment?'

'You don't. She's not. Is that all you came in to ask me?'

'You're a ruthless bastard,' she said with feeling.

'I've been called that before. It has quite a familiar ring to it. Why not try "arrogant swine"?'

'You've probably been called that too.' She was

determined to hold on to her temper, which she could feel rising rapidly.

'Very probably. But enough of this flattery. What is it you want me to tell you?'

'You already know. Why am I here?' She paused. 'And who hired you?' And she reached out her hand, resisting the urge to knock him senseless, and laid it gently on his cheek. 'Please,' she whispered, with a catch in her voice that should have melted the heart of any man.

He took hold of her hand for a moment, then moved it gently from his face. 'That was nice,' he remarked. 'Though I regret I must return it. You'll be giving me ideas if you do things like that, Joanna.' But his face was expressionless, his eyes held no spark of humanity. They were cold hard eyes, as cold and hard as he was, and he lay there, as though knowing, even at that physical disadvantage, that he had nothing to fear from her. He was mocking her, playing with her like a cat plays with a mouse, and she hated him more than she had ever hated anyone in her life—and there was nothing she could do about it.

She fought for control. It was all she could do to sit there normally. She felt herself trembling inwardly with anger at him, and took a deep breath, resisting all her natural impulses.

And he knew. He knew, that was the awful thing, for sudden sharp tension, as brilliant and dangerous as an electric shock, filled the room. He sat up abruptly, his face and eyes no longer impassive, but alert, wary—alive.

'Go and finish your siesta,' he said.

'No! You can't make me go.' Joanna jumped to her feet and looked around her, then picked up his sandal and hurled it at the window. It was a blazing gesture of hopeless defiance and anger. She whirled round on him as he rose to his feet, panther-like, and moved towards her.

'Don't touch me!' she panted, backing away from him. The sandal had only cracked the window through the light blind, and lay on the floor. She picked it up and threw it at him, but he deflected it with his arm, came to her, took hold of her, and shook her.

'Don't be so childish,' he grated. 'What are you trying to do? Wreck the place?'

'Yes!' She twisted from his grasp with a sharp upward and outward thrust of her arms, and kicked his kneecap hard, following it instantly with a flailing blow with her left arm which would probably have knocked him out if it had connected. It didn't, and a moment later she was held by him in a steel grip. It had all happened within seconds, so quick were both their reactions.

'My God,' he muttered, 'you're a vicious little bitch! You can thank your lucky stars you're a woman and not a man.'

Joanna was as lithe as a cat, and as swift. She relaxed, so that he loosened his hold on her, and freed herself, down, and away, wriggling, writhing, turned, and ran to the door. She never reached it. She was fast, but Roarke was faster still, and he caught her and slammed her against it, knocking the breath out of her, took hold of her, and kissed her.

It was a savage kiss, an insult, a violation, and she tried to scream, but his lips drowned the sound. Panting, breathless, when he was done, she glared at him helplessly, a prisoner in his arms, her mouth bruised, her mind shocked.

'Let me——' she began.

'Like hell I will,' he said thickly. 'I'd like to beat you.'

'Then try,' she panted. 'Just try it—you—you——' she couldn't find a word bad enough for him. He took her, flung her on to the bed, and pinioned her arms and legs down with his own.

'Now, escape—if you can,' he taunted. 'We'll see how strong you really are.'

Eyes blazing hatred, she said nothing, just looked at him, shaking with impotent rage. 'My God,' he said, 'the sooner he comes here the better. He's welcome to you, you little hellion. And heaven knows why he's bothered——'

'Who?' she shouted. *'Who?'* She was sobbing, because she couldn't move, and because her temper had evaporated swiftly in the shocks and struggles of this, the biggest battle of her life. 'Tell me—tell me——' her body was racked by sobs, the anger, all gone now, transmuted to a sorrow so deep that she could no longer contain it. She was weak, so weak that whatever he did now, she couldn't fight him. The tension too, that sharp electric atmosphere that had triggered off the epic struggle, had changed and was sharper—but different. The kiss had, in the strangest possible way, done that.

Joanna turned her head to one side, her arms still pinioned by Roarke, and shook helplessly. 'Don't you see—please see,' she sobbed, 'I can't bear it, not knowing. I was angry—but I'm so frightened and alone.'

Movement, soft, blurred movement as he eased himself away, and she was free, but she couldn't move. She lifted her hands to her face to hide it from him, for no one had seen her cry before, and she was scarcely aware of what she was saying. She was bruised, but more mentally than physically. She had reacted violently to him, and even in the midst of her pain now she realised that he had done no more than defend himself. He had done no more than that, yet he could have. He could have killed her, had he chosen, or broken her body as well as her spirit. The past seemed to open before her, empty hollow memories mingling with the images of the photographs, innocent enough in themselves but a damning indictment of her life style. And somehow it had all been leading up to this.

She closed her eyes and felt herself being lifted slightly, and held again, only this time very differently. There was all his strength and power there, but a gentleness as well, as he cradled her to his chest, arms around her, and her painful, body shaking sobs, died away.

She felt so safe. For the first time in her life she knew a feeling of utter warmth and security in another's arms. She raised her face to him, and his was blurred with her tears. 'I'm sorry,' she said. She never apologised to anyone. She had never needed or wanted to.

The kiss was as inevitable as time itself. It was gentle, and his mouth came down soft upon hers, and the hands that held her closely to him were a delight and not a prison. Glowing warmth filled her, and through her, him, and time was blurred, as were her senses, and her body was alive to his touch. They both moved and lay back, Roarke beside her now on the bed, bodies touching, she tingling, and he stroking and caressing and teasing in a way she had never known before.

She stroked his face with fingers that found the touch of him something wonderful, and she whispered: 'Forgive me.'

'There's nothing to forgive,' he murmured, and his eyes had lost their hardness, his face held tenderness. She had not seen him tender before, had not thought that he would be capable of being so. And she knew, in an instant of heart-stopping awareness, that she was falling in love with him, and the knowledge was a bitter-sweet pain. She smiled softly and moved her face to seek his lips like a child seeking warmth from the cold, and his mouth met hers in exquisite sensation, searching, fire in the blood. He held her closer still, but she could never be too close, and the contrast in his strength and gentleness now was a world away from what had gone before, and all the more wonderful for it.

He stroked her hair, his fingers making her head tingle, and she murmured helplessly, lost in delight. She had never known this before. No one had ever touched her like this. She slid her hands round his neck, revelling in the touch of strong shaggy hair, and again and again their lips met, and each time was different and more beautiful and perfect. She was both alive to everything, and at the same time languorous with the drugged sensation of love within her.

She wanted him to make love to her. She wanted him as she had never wanted a man before, and she knew, because all her instincts told her, that he would be a wonderful lover. Joanna had never made love in her life. She had never met a man she loved, or even liked sufficiently, to want to be with in the fullest sense of the word, but no one knew, save Joanna herself, for it was unfashionable to be a virgin in her world, and the men she had rejected had never told, for that would have been to lose face. And no one knew. Only Joanna, who had seen so much of promiscuity and had always regarded the activities of her friends with an amused tolerance, and never regarded herself as odd or different, knew that one day she would want to discover the oldest secret of all, and then she would, without a qualm.

And this was the time, the moment, the man. She drew him closer to her, her heart and senses pounding with the excitement that matched his. For he wanted her, she was quite sure of that, with her knowledge of him, so newly gained. His desire matched hers, his face blurred and softened with it, his arms tightening imperceptibly round her with each movement. She was truly his prisoner; prisoner of love, hearts beating as one heart, bodies aching with one desire, soon, soon, to be assuaged . . .

Then, shockingly, he was moving—but away. Away

from her, pulling himself free as though with an effort that cost him too dear. He sat there, as if in pain, and he was shaking. 'No,' he said huskily. 'I—didn't intend for things——'

Still drowsy with longing, Joanna didn't understand his words. They made no sense. Nothing was making sense. 'Roarke?' she said, and put her hand over the one that was fastening her dress. 'Roarke—I don't——'

'I promised.' He got to his feet, staggered slightly as he tried to move away, and she scrambled across the bed and knelt so that she was on a level with his chest. She put her hands out, to hold him, to tell him she knew not what, but he pushed at her as if not able to bear her touch. 'Don't,' he said. 'Don't you understand?' His voice was slurred, as if drunk, or drugged, or in pain. 'I promised your—I promised I would keep you safe, and safe doesn't include taking you into my bed and making love to you.'

She fell back, stunned, and he reached over for her, lifted her up, and took her in his arms. He held her in a controlled manner. The trembling had stopped. 'Don't make it more difficult for me,' he said.

'I want you,' she whispered. 'I've never wanted to make love——' she paused, but the words were nearly out, so she might as well finish the humiliation, 'with any man before——'

She heard his sharply indrawn breath, then, softly, almost like a sigh: 'Are you telling me——' He stopped, as if unable to say more.

'I've never been to bed with a man,' she said.

There was a long silence. Roarke seemed incapable of speech or movement. 'It's all right,' Joanna went on, bitter-voiced. 'I don't expect you to believe me. I've read the gossip columns too, you know. It just happens to be true.' She laughed. 'That's ironic, isn't it? Everyone thinks I've had a string of affairs, including all the men

I rejected. Each thought he was the only one left out, and kept quiet——' she paused. 'You're the first one I've ever told—and that two minutes after you more or less told me no, thanks!' She looked up at him. Drained now of all emotion, she couldn't even smile. Her skin felt tight and drawn. She thought she would never want to smile again. 'I'll get out of your room,' she said. 'Don't worry.' She turned to go and he caught her arm. She paused, not really wanting him to touch her any more. 'Please let me go,' she said quietly. 'I'd rather be alone, if you don't mind.'

She was under control, but only just. She ached all over, inside and out. There were new bruises now, to add to those she had deserved. But these were inside, and would never show. As Roarke released his hold on her arm, she added: 'I'm not going to try and escape any more, or even ask you again who made you bring me here. I'll wait. Perhaps I've already learned something, who knows?'

She turned then and walked away from him. 'Joanna,' he called quietly, but she didn't stop, or turn, or answer. She walked out of the door and went into her own room, and bolted the door after her.

At midnight, Joanna, who had remained in her room reading paperback books from the vast collection in the library downstairs, emerged from her exile and went down to the hall. She had eaten nothing all day, and she was faint with hunger.

Roarke was nowhere to be seen, nor the woman servant. Joanna had not even seen the man, and knew only that his name was Rojas. She went into the kitchen, which was equipped with a large freezer and an equally large refrigerator. The kitchen, too, was empty. Perhaps everyone had left. She wasn't sure if she cared. She wasn't sure about a lot of things any more, and she had

had plenty of time to think in the hours since the scene with Roarke.

He had come up to her room an hour or so afterwards and knocked, asking her if she was coming down to eat. She had told him no, she wasn't hungry, thank you. She had heard him walking away, and those had been their last words since.

She wondered if it were possible to die inside and still be alive on the outside, because that was exactly how she felt. The awful thing was that she didn't fully understand why. She found some fruit, and cut a piece of cheese from a plastic container in the refrigerator, put on water for coffee and sat down to eat while she waited for the water to boil.

It was there that Roarke found her minutes later. He walked in silently, and she turned and looked at him. 'I was hungry,' she explained.

'You would be.' It was as though nothing had happened. Except that he too had a wariness about him, a reserve. 'Is that water for coffee? Good, I'll have one as well.'

He found two cups and saucers, a jar of ground coffee, and spooned some into the percolator. Joanna sat and ate a few grapes, and watched him. He was different, very different. Not like he had been at the party, goading her into reaction with his softly barbed, clever words. Not aggressive as he had been after their arrival—and certainly, most definitely not like he had been after their explosive fight in the bedroom. She was seeing yet another facet of this deep, complex man who had abducted her, and it was even more puzzling.

He was like a remote stranger. An invisible wall was there, intangible, and yet, to Joanna, who was seeing him with eyes made perceptive with love, it was as real as though she could reach out and touch it.

'Have you eaten?' she asked, when she could no longer

bear the growing silence. Perhaps he didn't intend to speak unless she spoke first.

'Yes, a few hours ago.' That was all. Roarke put the coffee to percolate, then moved over to the refrigerator.

'Where are the Indian couple?'

He shrugged. 'In bed, I imagine. They get up early.'

She decided to see if he would speak without her having to ask a question first. She sat, and ate, and waited. He took cheese out, biscuits from a cupboard, set them on the table, fetched a knife and plate. His face was impassive, a carved mask of indifference. Anything was preferable to that. He made the coffee and put the two cupsful on the table, together with the sugar and tinned milk. Then he sat down. He looked at her, and it was like being stared at by a total stranger—except that Joanna was used to being stared at by total strangers wherever she went, and was completely unmoved by the experience. This was different. Emotionally shattered by the combination of everything that had happened, she was, for the first time in her life, feeling vulnerable and unsure.

She would have stared him out, or ignored him. She was good at doing both, normally. But this wasn't a normal time. It was like no time she had ever known, a dream, bordering on nightmare, and no idea how long it would last. For when the man arrived, what then?

He began to drink his coffee, and he took a biscuit and some cheese and put them on his plate. All in silence. 'All right,' said Joanna. 'Is this some part of a punishment?'

He looked up. 'What do you mean?'

'The silence. Am I getting the silent treatment?'

'Do you want to talk?' His face was expressionless, his eyes frighteningly dark and blank.

'You know damed well what I mean!' Her voice was rising.

'I know that you're getting upset about something. I'm not sure what it is—but then I don't know you, do I?'

'You should do. You nearly made love to me this afternoon, or have you forgotten?' she demanded.

Roarke's expression didn't alter. 'I've not forgotten,' he answered, and he watched her, waiting for her next words, but she had none. She rubbed her right wrist, where a bruise had begun to appear. He had done that when he had held her. She didn't know what to do or say next. The food she was trying to eat tasted like ashes. She couldn't swallow any more. The feeling of being in a prison was so strong that it nearly overwhelmed her.

'I want to go outside and get some fresh air,' she said at last.

'That's impossible. It's after midnight, it's pitch dark—and it's dangerous.'

'I'll go alone if you're frightened,' she snapped.

'You won't go anywhere tonight. In the morning perhaps. Now—no.'

'I suppose the doors are locked?'

'Of course.'

'Then I might as well go to bed.'

'You might as well,' he agreed.

Joanna stood up and picked up her coffee cup. For a moment she was tempted ... But she had learned one lesson. Physical attack earned swift response. Roarke didn't work by anyone's rules save his own, and she didn't like them, but she had to abide by them if she was to retain any vestiges of self-respect. She turned and walked out of the room.

'Goodnight,' he said, but she neither paused nor answered on her way out.

The rain woke her early from a restless and dream-filled sleep, and she lay for a moment or two not recognising the drumming, rattling sounds as she surfaced from a nightmare that was even now receding into oblivion. She padded to the window and drew back the curtains, to be met by a grey wall of water. It streamed down the windows, blurring the glass, making it impossible to see anything save a grey darkness outside.

Further sleep was impossible, and it would soon be dawn. Joanna felt wretched. She stumbled to her bathroom and ran a warm shower, and washed her hair. Her head throbbed, her body ached, her eyes burned with fatigue. She wondered if she were ill, and prayed not. To be a healthy prisoner was one thing; to be sick, and dependent upon the ministrations of Roarke or the silent Indian woman, would be unthinkable.

She dressed in a blouse and skirt of pale lemon shades, washed her previous day's clothes and hung them on the shower rail to drip dry. Then she went down to the library. She found a stack of writing paper that she had noticed on her previous day's visit, sat down at the desk, and began to write. There was little else to do. Joanna had never kept a diary in her life—she had never had time—but an idea had taken hold the previous night, and it appealed to her. She would keep an account of what had happened to her—strictly for her eyes only—in diary form. She wasn't even sure how to begin, but once she had forced herself to make a start, the words poured out on to the paper, and there was a kind of release in writing.

She was surprised to find that she had covered several sheets of paper when her concentration was disturbed by the entrance of Roarke to the library. He stood in the doorway. 'I've made breakfast in the kitchen,' he told her. She gathered up the sheets of paper, and the pen, and put them in her evening bag, and looked at him. She was pleased to see that he seemed to have slept badly as well.

'You have?' she answered. 'That's nice. Where's the Indian woman?'

'I don't know,' he answered.

She stood up, picking up her bag. 'What do you mean, you don't know? I thought she lived here with her husband?'

'She does, but she's gone, and so has he, and their bed hasn't been slept in.' He said the words in a calm, matter-of-fact way, and Joanna gaped at him.

'Do they often do that?' she asked. 'Simply vanish?'

He shrugged. 'I haven't a clue—although I wouldn't have thought so. All I know is that we're alone.'

That fact had already occurred to Joanna. It wouldn't make much difference. She had only met the woman for a few minutes at breakfast the previous morning. She was no less, or more, of a prisoner for the Indians having gone.

'What about the birds in the aviary?' she asked. 'Who will feed them?'

'That had occurred to you too, had it? I've already checked them, before I made breakfast. They need little help from us. The plants are specially grown for their nourishment, and there's an ingenious arrangement that collects rainwater in there. They could safely be left for a week or more.'

'Why are you telling me this?' Her bag wouldn't close, but she paused in the act of trying to shut it, alerted by something odd in his tone, and what he had said.

'You'd better come and eat,' he answered, and that was no answer at all, but she sensed it was all she was going to get until she was in the kitchen, so she followed him out. He had laid the table, and the percolator was bubbling merrily, and he moved about calmly getting food, producing finally a bowl of what looked like sour cream. 'Yoghurt,' he told her, 'and delicious. Help yourself to it.'

They were both sitting eating before he spoke again. Joanna had decided that she wasn't going to ask him anything at all. He would either tell her of his own accord or she would not find out his reasons for the information on the birds. That was the way she felt now. There was already a sense of unreality about the whole situation. Not much else could happen, and if it did, so what? she thought. Her life had already been irrevocably changed in the past forty-eight hours. Nothing would ever be quite the same again, and Joanna was becoming inured to shocks and surprises.

Roarke regarded her steadily across the table. 'I have something to tell you,' he began. She lifted one eyebrow slightly but said nothing. He was quite likely to tell her to wait until after breakfast to hear what it was, she decided, if she dared to ask.

'Really?' she remarked at last.

'There's been a slight hitch in the arrangements.'

'Mmm?' She licked some melting butter from her finger.

'The person who—is coming has been delayed.'

'What—how?' She forgot her resolve.

'I was contacted by radio early this morning. He's been taken ill.'

'Am I supposed to feel sorry about that?' she asked with a trace of bitterness.

'You might if you know who it is.'

'But I don't—so I don't, if you see what I mean. All *I* feel is anger at this stupidity. I'm supposed to be in Rio de Janeiro—though I don't suppose *you* give a damn about that.' Joanna felt her face go pink with temper.

'Don't worry, I'm going to tell you in a minute—but there's something more; something—worse.'

'Surprise me!' she snapped.

'Something is wrong. Here—outside. I don't know what it is, but I sensed it last night. Finding Rojas and his wife gone only made it more definite in my mind. I smell trouble, and believe me, I have an instinct for these things.'

She was stilled. She didn't doubt it, not for an instant. Her heart beat faster, but she kept her face calm. Joanna was no coward. To fight frustration and anger, and an invisible resentment, was one thing. To be faced with a reality of trouble was quite something else. She nodded.

'I believe you. You'd need a sixth sense of that kind in your job. That's why you told me about the birds, isn't it?'

'Yes,' he answered.

'Because we might have to leave suddenly?'

'I hope not—but yes, it might happen.'

She shrugged. 'This isn't exactly the South American holiday I'd envisaged, but it makes a change.'

'Have I frightened you?'

She gave him a scornful glance. 'I don't frighten easily, Roarke. Disappointed?'

'No. Nor surprised.'

'Oh. You expected me to give a girlish laugh and say "how super!" did you?'

'Not exactly.' He regarded her very seriously across the table. His face was hard. 'But knowing the man who's been delayed, no, I'm not surprised you've reacted as you have.'

'I don't see the connection,' she shrugged.

'You will. The man is a relative of yours.'

Whatever she had expected, it wasn't that. She felt the blood drain from her face. 'A—relative?' she whispered. 'A *relative*?'

'Someone you thought had died years ago.'

Joanna shook her head slowly, hurting, aching. She was icily cold, as though drenched in the deadening rain that lashed mercilessly down outside. Her mouth twisted. 'A—a—ah——' she made anguished sounds, the blood pounding in her head, and unable to control her hands or face. Her arms had gone weak, and tingled, and she felt as if someone had struck her hard.

Roarke moved swiftly and came round to her side of the table and put his hands firmly on her arms, steadying her from the dreadful trembling that shook her entire body.

'Joanna,' he said urgently, 'listen to me. You thought your father had died, lost at sea, when you were a baby. He didn't. He's very much alive. The man who had you brought here, by me, is your father.'

# CHAPTER FOUR

JOANNA's head went back, and she would have fallen had it not been for Roarke's restraining arms. She felt herself being lifted, and lay limply against him as he carried her out of the kitchen and into the drawing room where he laid her carefully down on the settee, putting a cushion beneath her head for support. He rubbed her hands, kneeling beside her as she struggled to remain conscious.

'Roarke,' she whispered, 'is it true?'

'It is true.'

'My father didn't die?'

'No. He owns this house. He lives here most of the year. This is why it was ideal, when you were in Manaos—can you hear me, Joanna?'

'I can hear you,' she murmured. The trembling had stopped, and life was returning to her shocked system. She took a deep, shuddering breath. 'This isn't a sick joke, is it?'

'It isn't a joke at all. Now you know why I didn't intend to tell you. But circumstances have changed. I had no choice.'

'I don't understand anything——' she began.

'You will—when you see him.'

'Where is he?'

'He's in Rio.'

'Where I'm supposed to be.'

'Would you have believed it if a man had come up to you in the street and told you he was your father?'

'No. May I have something to drink, please?'

'Sure, I'll get you a drop of brandy.' He left her side

and returned with a small glass. 'Sip that slowly.'

Joanna felt the colour returning to her ashen face as she sipped. She took a deep breath. 'I shouldn't have lost control,' she said with dignity, at last.

He took the empty glass from her. 'You've had quite a few shocks these past few hours. Stay there, I'm going to do something now, before it's too late. I'm going to move the helicopter. If there is trouble—and there may well be, it's no damned use to us where it is.'

'But where to?'

'The roof is flat, and reinforced at the back. It wasn't necessary to park there when we came. Now it is.'

He went out, and after a few moments Joanna stood and went to the window and watched. She could see little, save the incessant, driving rain, blurred movement, as of a giant bird lifting, an eerie sight. It was impossible for her to simply wait. She ran up the stairs and along the passage leading to the aviary. There came movement overhead, muffled footsteps, and she looked up to see a hatch opening up in the ceiling ahead of her. A drenched, almost unrecognisable man jumped down. Roarke was soaked to the skin.

'I thought I told you to wait,' he said, taking off his squelching sandals.

She managed a faint smile. 'I don't always obey orders,' she said.

'Nor you do. I'm going to strip off, I'm soaked through.'

'I'll wait downstairs,' she said quickly, and fled.

She locked and bolted the front door and went into the drawing room again. Roarke had spoken of trouble; she had accepted his awareness of it. But of what kind—and from which direction? If this place was as remote as she feared, then who in their right mind would build a house there? She already knew the answer to that. Her father. Her own father, whom she had never known.

She felt a surge of such emotion that it was almost overwhelming. What would he look like? There were so many questions, too many, tumbling round in her head. But the knowledge was a warm glow, that was the most important thing. It was wonderful, and awesome, both at the same time. And she loved Roarke, who had brought her here. That, too, was right.

She went to meet him as he came down the stairs, dry again, clad in jeans and white tee-shirt. The short sleeves showed his heavily muscled arms, the broad chest and shoulders. He had brought her here, and now, knowing at last why, she absolved him of all blame.

She went up to him and stood in front of him. 'I think we ought to have a talk,' she said.

'Let's sit down first.' He followed her into the drawing room. She was seeing everything with new eyes. It was no longer just a stranger's house. It had become a different place. Her father's house, his furniture, his pictures. She had no ideas about him, she had never known anything about him at all, but the room told her much about the kind of man he must be, and she drank in the atmosphere as she looked around her, and a strange feeling was in her. Whatever happened, now or later, she had this much. She had something.

Roarke remained standing by the window, tall and still, but as alert as any jungle animal. He knew what she was doing. 'Will you tell me about him, please?' she asked simply.

'He's in his late fifties, well built, about my height— grey-haired. He's got your eyes, Joanna. He's full of humour, and he cares about a lot of things that most people expect others to worry about—conservation, life, peace, endangered species—and he doesn't just sit back and talk about it, he does something. He was on Operation Greenpeace with the boat that effectively stopped a seal cull in Canada a couple of years ago.

He's travelled the world on missions that would daunt lesser people—and he's succeeded. Your father is no ordinary man, Joanna.' He turned slowly towards her.

A picture was emerging, strange and wonderful, like nothing she had ever known. Of a man very different from those her life normally touched. 'You admire him, don't you?' she asked.

His mouth curved slightly. 'He's one of the very few people I do admire in this world, yes.' He looked steadily at her. 'And now you know why I did what I did.'

'Only we seem to be in difficulties,' she remarked, standing up and going over to where he was at the window.

'We could be. Time will tell.'

She followed his glance. Very little could be seen outside. The torrential rain was easing, and the ground was a quagmire, and the sentinel trees were a dark wall that stretched around the house, effectively imprisoning them both. 'We're stuck here, just the two of us.' Joanna said it without bitterness. The different kinds of shocks had left her numbed and rather remote from everything. Something inside her reached out to the silent man by her side. Perhaps, after all, this was what her life had been leading up to all these years. This remote place, waiting for a man who was her father. It would be ironic if she were never to see him. 'I'm not afraid of anything,' she added. It was perfectly true, and the words came out with simple directness, and she turned to face him at the same moment that he turned to look at her. Something—some awareness, reached out to enfold them both, like a warm cloak. There were three words, even more simple and direct, that would have told him why she was not afraid, if she had dared to say them. But they would remain forever unsaid, she knew that. The three most beautiful words in the world: I love you. Love would not be a word in Roarke's vocabulary. She knew that just as surely as she knew her own inner feelings for him. 'You never told me if Roarke is your first or second name,' she murmured, after a moment of silence.

'My surname. My first is Adam.'

Adam Roarke. It suited him. It seemed so logical and right that she felt faintly surprised that she hadn't guessed. 'But you're always called Roarke? Even by my father?' How strange it was to say 'my father' like that. She had never done so before. She tasted the words, my father. My father, my father, in silent wonder.

'Yes.'

'How long have you known him?' she asked.

'Eight or nine years.'

'Tell me how you met.'

'We met in London when he married my cousin Olivia.'

She hadn't expected that. 'He's—married?' she whispered.

'Yes, he is.'

'And my—stepmother——' it was difficult to say, although there was no reason why there should be, none at all. 'Is she with him now?'

'Yes, Joanna. It was she who contacted me.'

She took a deep breath. 'How? Contacted, I mean?'

'There's a radio transmitter here. I haven't told her that Rojas and his wife are gone. She's got enough to worry about without that.'

'How ill is he?' she asked.

'He had appendicitis. Nothing serious, thank God, but it could take days before he's fit enough to fly here.'

'By helicopter?'

Roarke smiled faintly. 'It's the only way to travel, Joanna.' The atmosphere was like nothing that had ever been before. There was an acute awareness of him on her part, and she knew without any vestige of doubt that it was mutual. It was as if her perceptions were sharpened to a degree she had never known, and they were truly alone, together in a wilderness that he had brought her to against her wishes—and she would not have chosen different.

She should have been in Rio now, joining in the festivities with thousands of others, staying with Brazilian friends who had an apartment on Copacabana Beach, searching, always searching for she knew not what in a relentless and reckless merry-go-round of pleasure and excitement. Instead of which she stood by a window and looked out on to a steady grey downpour, with no escape, waiting to meet a man who, an hour previously, she had not known existed—and she was more alive now than she had ever been.

'I know why you hate me,' she said suddenly, because it was time it was said. 'You think I'm a hard, selfish bitch. You're right. I have been for years—but something has changed in these last few hours. You'll see.'

'You're probably right,' he answered, and it was as though he were touching her, even though he was a foot away, hands at sides. The air was vibrant with tension, reaching out, encompassing both of them. 'But I don't hate you. I don't waste emotion on hating anybody.' He was saying the words, and she was hearing them, and that was on the surface, but there were other, unspoken words between them, and she didn't know what they were, only that she felt almost dizzy, her skin tingling with a heady awareness of him. She wanted to move away, but she was held as if by invisible threads binding them together. Then, slowly, he turned, and put one hand on her arm. The shock was electric. She caught her breath, looking at him, eyes wide. His eyes had gone very dark, full upon her, his mouth curving sensuously, his very breath seeming to touch her face. She stood still, not trying to move away, for that would be to let him know her secret; that she might not be afraid of any outside dangers, but she was afraid of his nearness and what it did to her.

'You're trembling,' he said.

'It's nothing,' she murmured. 'Just delayed shock. I've had a few——'

'Yes.' But he didn't take his hand away. It burned her arm. He lifted his other hand slowly and put it on her other arm. 'I'll protect you.'

'I—know you will.' She moistened her lips with her tongue. She no longer wanted to move away. This was more than enough. Roarke's touch was more than enough. A kind of magnetism flowed from him, filling her senses, drowning her in the awareness of him. His eyes were upon her mouth, her neck, her breast, lingering in a caress that said more than words could do. Don't you see, she wanted to say, it doesn't matter as long as we're together—and perhaps he could read her mind, for it was as though he heard, and as though the unspoken answer came; I know, I know.

She could no longer look at him, or he would know even more from her eyes. She dropped her glance, staring instead at the buttons on his shirt. All this had happened within moments, but it might have been an eternity, so powerful was the heady sensation. There were so many questions she wanted to ask, but she couldn't break the fragile spell that bound them. Dear God, she thought, I want him so much, and he'll never know—or perhaps he does—and her heart thudded, pounding in her ears, and she had to fight to keep standing. Hold me, she said silently, hold me, for I'm afraid, but it's of myself, not of you, or any marauders outside.

He released her and turned away and the spell was broken. He had answered her unspoken plea, and she knew why. He was a man, after all. She didn't doubt a very virile one, and he had made a promise to her father, one of the few men in the world that he admired, and he wasn't going to break it. 'When it's darker, this evening, I'll go and scout around outside,' he said. 'You'll stay here. Can you use a gun?'

'Yes.'

'I'm not suggesting you'll need one, but it's only common sense to be prepared.' His tone was practical, very matter-of-fact, and dismissive of all that had happened. But what had, after all? Nothing. They had stood at the window looked out, she had asked, and he had answered, several questions, no more.

She made her tone equally casual. 'I don't want to shoot you by mistake,' she said. 'We'd better have some signal for when you return.'

'Don't worry.' He gave a wry smile. 'There's a concealed way out. Let me show you now.'

A locked door led off from the kitchen. Roarke opened it and steps went down to what appeared to be a wine cellar. He went first, Joanna following, treading cautiously in the darkness. Then hard earth beneath her feet and ahead a narrow passage at the end of which he stopped and held out his hand in the gloom for her to take. He pulled her slightly forward and made her touch the door, which, she then discovered, had three bolts.

'There's a hidden path outside, covered by shrubs,' he said quietly. He spoke in a completely impersonal manner. There was absolutely nothing in his voice of what had gone before. 'When I return, I'll knock twice, pause, then once. Got that?'

'Yes,' she answered, shivering. It was cold and dank down there.

'Let's go back. After you.' She felt her way along clay walls and reached the steps. She stumbled going up, unfamiliar with the steps, and he caught and steadied her. 'Careful! Tonight we'll have a torch.'

'Yes, good idea.' They reached the kitchen. Joanna brushed cobwebs from her dress and arms, and he laughed. 'What is it?' she asked.

'You've got a long smudge on your cheek. Stay still.' He came to her and rubbed with his fingers, not hard, quite gently. 'That's it.'

'Thanks.' She turned away. 'What do we do now?'

'Not much *to* do—except wait. The rain's stopping and the ground will be dry soon. I'd rather you didn't venture outside. In fact I'll put it more strongly—don't.'

'I wouldn't. I don't mind dangers I can see, but not——' she hesitated.

'Not the invisible ones?' he prompted, and she nodded. 'Look, Joanna, this may be all my imagination, do you understand?'

She looked shrewdly at him. 'If I thought for a moment that it was, I'd say so.'

'And you don't?'

'No. I accept your—sixth sense about such things.'

'But you're not scared?'

'I already told you. No, I'm not.' This was a practical discussion, and quite a world away from the one before. He nodded.

'Looks like we're in partnership. In which case——' it was his turn to hesitate, 'I'd better tell you what I plan. Night time is obviously a period of greater danger than now. I intend to remain awake all night, and I suggest you do as well. And that means us sleeping during the day.'

'Easier said than done,' she answered dryly.

'I agree. Which is why I'm going to rest now. You're obviously wide awake. So am I, but I can make myself sleep any time, anywhere. I'm going to have a hot shower and go to bed for, say, four hours. Will you wake me at noon?'

'Yes, I'll keep watch.'

'But you won't venture out?'

'No, I promise.'

He nodded. 'Okay. Twelve o'clock. Then it's your turn.'

'Yes.' Joanna watched him go with strangely mixed feelings. Then she busied herself tidying the kitchen.

Roarke woke her up at five o'clock in the afternoon from a deep sleep with a cup of strong coffee. 'It'll be dark soon,' he told her as she sat up in bed, still drowsy. 'Drink that up.' He had dressed all in black again, and wore a holster on a belt at his waist. There was a gun in the holster. He saw her involuntary glance at it, and grimaced, then sat on the bed.

'I don't imagine I'll need it.'

'I'm sure not—but be careful——'

'I will. I can move silently when I need to. I found a torch. When I go, you bolt the door after me and wait in the kitchen. You'll hear me knock from there.'

Joanna was drinking the coffee, fully wakened by now, and she nodded. She had slipped on her nightdress when she had gone to bed, and it was a very respectable, even demure, cotton affair, more concealing than any of the dresses. 'Let me have a shower and get dressed, will you?' she asked. 'I won't take more than ten minutes.'

'Of course.' He stood up, the large, brooding, potentially violent man, now as calm as she had ever known him. He was a strange, complex mixture, she thought. Completely impersonal, like a stranger—which, after all, was precisely what he was. She didn't know him at all, but she loved him, and ached for him, and she was getting as adept as he at concealing her feelings. He had come into her life and changed it completely in less than three days, and perhaps he was aware of that. But he would never be aware of her innermost feelings, because she didn't intend him to be.

When her father came, Roarke would leave. He had already told her that he had commitments elsewhere. 'Don't you have people waiting for you?' she asked, as she finished her coffee.

He shrugged. 'Yes, but it can't be helped. There's no way I can reach them.'

'Doesn't it worry you?'

He looked at her with dark thoughtful eyes. 'I never worry about what I can't alter. The only alternative is to go, and for the moment we're staying. For obvious reasons.'

'But you must let my father—and stepmother—know soon. I mean, they mustn't come here if there's danger——'

'Mustn't they? Do you think he'd keep away if he knew?' He smiled slightly. 'He's lived through worse——'

'But he's not well——'

'He will be. He may leave Olivia behind, but I'd be surprised if she let him. She's a very determined woman. They don't come alone, either. Your father has two male assistants who are well used to living in the wilds. No, Joanna, I'll be contacting them tomorrow to see how your father is, and I'll put my cousin fully in the picture then. What she tells him is up to her, dependent on his condition.'

'It'll be like the cavalry to the rescue,' she said lightly.

'Something like that,' he agreed in dry tones. He picked up her empty cup. 'I'll leave you to get ready.' And he went out.

Joanna ran a shower, stripped and had a leisurely wash. She dressed in a clean dress, put on the sandals, combed her hair, and was ready. They had eaten well at noon, and she wasn't hungry.

When she went down Roarke was ready to go out, and waiting for her, black-clad, gun at waist, black track shoes. A dark frightening figure. He handed her a torch. 'Go first,' he told her. 'Practise for when you let me in.'

'Yes.' Her heart was beating faster. She didn't want him to go, but how foolish it would be to say it. She was frightened for him, not for herself. When they reached the door, she unbolted it, and the bolts were well oiled and easy to move. As it swung silently open, she whispered: 'Take care.'

He grinned briefly at her, but said nothing. A moment later he had vanished like a shadow into the darkness. Joanna bolted the door and made her way back. She had no idea how long he would be. Her role was to wait. That was all—but she knew she would rather have been with him.

She busied herself preparing a meal, finding a chicken in the freezer, and cutting it, with great difficulty, and with the aid of a razor-sharp knife, into four quarters. She seasoned the joints and put them into a roasting pan. All the time she was working, images of what would be happening now in Rio came to her. She knew, because she had been there the previous year for the Mardi Gras festivities. The streets would be filled with noise, music, colour, and multitudes of brightly dressed floats, and carnival dragons, and weird monsters, and masked merrymakers, and she would have been in the thick of it with her Brazilian friends, and excitement would have been at fever pitch.

No greater contrast could be imagined between those images and the reality of what was happening to her now. She was working in a kitchen, something totally alien to her, preparing food for a man who might or might not return.

She began to think about her father's reasons for having her brought by Roarke to the house, and while he obviously could not have envisaged trouble, she thought she had an inkling of his motives. His timing, although he could not know it, had been perfect. For Joanna to be deprived of one of the high spots of her year would normally have incensed her beyond reason. Something had changed drastically—something that neither he nor she could have imagined.

She wanted desperately to meet her father. More immediate, though, was the thought of Roarke, somewhere out there in the alien world of the night and the jungle. Joanna's heart was heavy with apprehension, and fear filled her with a pain so that she couldn't think clearly any more. She forced herself to work, cleaning kitchen surfaces that already gleamed, sweeping the stone-flagged floor and then washing it. And all the time her ears were alert for the slightest sound from anywhere in the house—but especially from the cellar. At lunchtime Roarke had shown her the gun he was leaving for her; a Browning automatic, large, heavy—and loaded.

It was on the table near her. She had used one before, on an army firing range, and was well aware of the kickback—and Joanna was as deadly accurate with a gun as with everything else. She regarded it now, and prayed she would not have to use it.

The worst time of all came then. She had no more to occupy her restless hands; all the work was done. She dared not wander far from the kitchen in case she didn't hear Roarke's knock, and all she could do was wait. And wait. And wait. Two hours passed, perhaps more, and every minute became an eternity for her. She paced the kitchen silently, like a cat, so as not to make a sound that might cover his knock, and she had never known such a dreadful time. Her dress clung to her and she longed for a shower, but she would not leave the kitchen. She found herself clenching her hands so tightly that the nails dug into her palms, and her stomach ached with the lump of fear that lay within it.

She sat down, then jumped up again and resumed pacing. Her vivid imagination provided pictures she didn't need or want, but they refused to go away. Pictures of Roarke lying somewhere injured, hurt—unable to get back, needing help—needing *her*—'Stop it,' she whispered fiercely. 'Stop it, stop it!'

So keyed up was she that the knock, when it came at last, did not at first register. Then, realising, she grabbed the torch, scrambled down the steps, and ran to the door. Her nerves were at screaming pitch. She opened it and he came in and bolted it after him. Overwhelming relief flooded her—followed by intense reaction so great that she exclaimed hotly:

'It took you long enough!'

'Thanks,' he answered drily, took the torch from her and went ahead of her up the steps and into the lighted kitchen which was filled by the aroma of roasting chicken and herbs. He turned to her, slammed the door shut behind her, and looked at her. 'I've come home to some welcomes in my time, but that was really something,' he said, face hard and dark.

'I was *worried*!' she stormed, hating him, now that he was safely back, for putting her through the hell of the last hours.

'Yes, you really sound it,' he answered, and took off his gun-belt, hanging it on a door hook. His voice was filled with irony. 'Where the hell do you think I've been? To the local pub for a couple of pints with the boys? There isn't one. Sorry to disappoint you—I've been merely sidling round trees in the pitch bloody darkness—still, you don't want to hear about *me*, I'm sure. How have you been filling *your* time, sweetie—doing some knitting?'

The raw, naked tension filled the room, anger on both sides, she not understanding, and hating hers, sparked off as it had been by overwhelming fear for him. His reaction—possibly also because of what he must have been through—was as swift and harsh, even harsher, than her own. They stared at each other, a foot or so apart, not touching, looking, challenging each other with angry eyes. Joanna wanted to cry out that she was sorry; she wanted too, to touch him, to hold him—but it was too late for that. There stretched between them a gulf so wide that nothing would bridge it. It needed only two words: I'm sorry, but her throat closed with tension, and she could not say them. She turned on her heel and ran out of the room, and her eyes were filled with the tears she would die rather than let him see.

She went up and sat on her bed after splashing her face and arms with cold water. The tension that had filled her drained away, leaving her completely exhausted. This should never have happened. It had all gone wrong. She sat there, rubbing her arms and knowing she must go down and tell him. It seemed to happen nearly every time they spoke, as though their nearness sparked off something that neither could help. He had denied that he hated her, but he certainly didn't like her. He liked and admired her father, and, for him, had brought Joanna here. But his opinion of her and her life style had been made only too plain. He felt contempt for her. And what else must he feel now? She rubbed her aching throat, raw with unshed tears. 'I'm sorry,' she whispered, but there was no one to hear. It was time to go. Now or never.

She ran down into the kitchen where he sat eating chicken, and she said: 'I'm sorry, Roarke—it was because I was so worried—reaction——'

He looked up. 'Try not to get too worried in future, will you? I don't think I could take *too* much of your concern.' And he looked back down at his plate and sliced a piece of chicken up. Joanna sat down. He wasn't making this easy.

'Is the chicken all right?' she asked.

He glanced up briefly. 'Fine.' That was all. He started eating again.

Joanna took a deep breath. 'All right, say it! I'm a stupid, hysterical bitch who can't control herself.'

'I don't need to. You just said it for me,' he rejoined drily. 'But yes, you are. I thought you were the cool one, well in control of every situation, the sophisticated jet-setter. I dare say you are, when everything's going *your* way. The trouble with life, Joanna, is that it doesn't *always* revolve round you, and the sooner you realise it the better.' He gave her a hard cool assessing look. 'One day, if a miracle happens, you might grow up. I won't be around to see it, and I can't say I'm bothered.'

If anyone else had said these things to her—if *he* had—only a day or so previously, she would have retaliated with a swift, cutting response. Instead she took a deep breath. 'Thanks,' she said wryly. Then: 'Did you see or hear anything outside?'

There was a brief pause before he answered. 'No, it's quiet. Possibly too quiet, I don't know. No animal sounds and no sign of life within a good radius of the house. It's going to be a waiting game. In the morning, before dawn, I'll go out again. And when you let me in, I expect a different reaction from you. I hope I make myself clear?'

'Yes.' She got up and went to serve herself with chicken and vegetables. She didn't feel particularly hungry, but it was important to eat and keep up strength. Roarke had already finished, and walked out as she sat down again. She heard him moving about upstairs, and a door closed.

The fireworks would be going off all over Rio, filling the sky with star bursts of colour and splendour. The noise would be deafening, people dancing frenziedly in the streets, streamers snaking through the air, confetti, balloons, laughter and music everywhere as inhibitions were thrown aside with convention. Here, there was silence; a restless, electric silence, filling the house, and her, with tension. And somewhere in Rio, away from the noise and crowds, lay her father, the reason she was here instead of there. The man her mother had said was dead. She must have had her reasons, but Joanna couldn't imagine what they could be. She felt as if she had been betrayed, and the hurt went deep. She had never thought she could be hurt by anyone, but she was learning fast. The knowledge brought her no pleasure, only a continuation of pain. She had also thought that she would never love any man sufficiently to be hurt, but that too had happened. She loved Roarke, and the love brought her pain, not joy. There was nothing she could do about that.

Once the link was established with her father, Roarke would go. Their worlds had never crossed before, and certainly would not do so in the future. She could no more imagine him swanning round on the deck of a luxury yacht than she could see herself scrabbling for emeralds in the Colombian earth. Soon he would be forgotten, she would try and make sure of that. But whether she would approach her world of parties and jet-setting with the same feelings was something she no longer felt sure about. Already so many things had receded from her mind, blurred, all mingling so that it was difficult to remember the most recent events. She sighed; self-pity was alien to her, and she fought it off. There was one sure antidote to that: work. She found dusters and polishes and went into the drawing room and started something she had never wanted or needed to do before—housework.

She was busily engaged in putting a lustrous shine on an antique table, concentrating exclusively on her task, all other thoughts pushed firmly away, when she was surprised by Roarke's voice from the doorway, and looked up, face flushed with exertion, hair tousled.

'Pity I've no camera,' he drawled, and came forward to inspect the surface of the table. Joanna pushed a strand of hair out of her eyes.

'You'd probably have something scathing to say if I was sitting reading a book,' she answered. 'So why don't you carry on doing whatever it is you're doing, and let me get on with my work?'

He nodded. 'Fair comment. You've missed a bit there.' He pointed. 'But for a beginner, you're not doing so badly.' She didn't know why she did what she did next. She would never know, except that she had taken more than enough. She stepped round the table swiftly, and hit him hard.

# CHAPTER FIVE

'YOU patronising *swine*!' she breathed, trembling with a mixture of relief and anger. Relief from the sudden release from her tortured thoughts, anger at him for everything he was. She no longer cared what he might do in retaliation. He did nothing. He looked at her, but he didn't move. It was as if he too knew what had driven her to her action.

His words confirmed it. 'Feel better now?' He stroked the cheek that she had hit, thoughtfully. 'Don't worry, I'm not going to hit you back.' He looked her slowly up and down, then smiled.

'Why don't you get out?' she demanded.

'Because I'm staying here. I have work to do as well— paperwork. I might as well do it in here.'

'In that case, I'll move.' Joanna picked up her cloth and tin of polish. 'I don't intend to sit doing nothing. I'll find somewhere else——'

'You have changed, haven't you?' he remarked. 'Is this how danger affects you?'

Her mouth twisted. 'I wouldn't expect *you* to understand,' she retorted scathingly. 'And I don't care one way or the other. I'll keep out of your way, don't worry.'

She stalked past him and went into the kitchen and he followed her. 'You can make me a coffee if you will,' he said. 'Hot, black and sweet.'

'And if I won't?'

'Then I'll make my own. I intend to keep awake all night, or had you forgotten that?'

'I'll make it.' She banged the kettle down on the stove.

70

'Thank you.' His tone was very dry. 'Bring it into the drawing room.' He walked out. I must be mad, Joanna thought. Yesterday, I'd have told him to go to hell. She felt confused, and her head ached with the tension. It was the waiting, the not knowing, that was doing it. It must be the same for him, even harder, for on him rested the responsibility for her protection. Joanna tried to think herself into his mind, and it was a salutary experience. Of course the pressures were far greater. She had been thinking only from her own point of view. *Her* worry at his long disappearance. *Her* own dismay at his anger. Roarke had been the one to go out into the night, not she—and he would go again, using all his skills at moving silently and secretly in dangerous jungle. Joanna bit her lip. And how had she greeted him? 'It took you long enough.' She groaned. His reaction, in retrospect, had been mild. And now, to compound it all, she had just given him a stinging slap across his face.

She made the coffee, poured his out carefully, added sugar, and took it in to him. He was sitting at a small writing desk by the shuttered windows. Joanna found a mat and placed the coffee on it. The desk was filled with papers, he was busy writing, and he didn't look up.

'Thanks,' he said, dismissal in the word.

'Roarke——' she ventured, and he looked up.

'What?'

'Do you want any help?'

'No. Why? Are you offering?' He didn't seem remotely interested.

'Yes, but only if you need me to.'

'I don't. I'm writing a report on my last expedition to Machu Picchu. It wouldn't interest you.'

'A report? An official one, do you mean?'

'No. For my own benefit—to go into a book eventually. Satisfied?'

Joanna shook her head. 'I can type it out if you'd like me to.'

'Type? You can *type*?' he sounded amused.

She took a deep breath. 'I learned it once, yes. I don't do too badly.'

His mouth quirked. 'It might give you something to do to keep you quiet. There's a typewriter and paper in the library. Can you imagine why?'

'I noticed before. No, why?'

'Your father has written books on South America.'

'He has?' It was a revelation to her. 'Are any here?'

'There may be.' He stood up. 'I'll go and fetch the machine in here. We'll stay in this room all night. It's central, we can hear any sounds, and it's better to remain together.'

'Yes. I'll come with you and have a look for one of his books.'

'As you wish.'

She searched the shelves—and then realised something. She turned to him as he gathered papers together. 'Roarke, what is my father's name?'

He looked up as if stunned. 'Don't you *know*?'

'I—thought—I think his first name is John. But I've only ever known my surname as Crozier. I suppose I just assumed it was his as well.' She felt foolish and vulnerable—and strangely sad, for something lost.

'My God,' he said softly, with feeling. 'It's John Cunningham.'

Even as he said the words she saw the name on the hard cover of a book and lifted it down. '*Some Birds of the Amazon*. John E. Cunningham,' she read. She opened it slowly, then, heart beating faster, turned to the back inside flap. A man looked out at her, tanned, silver-haired, with laughing mouth and eyes. He seemed to be looking directly at her. She blinked, and a tear fell on to the shiny paper and rolled down. This, this was her father. 'Oh,' she said softly. It was all she could say.

She heard Roarke move, heard his footsteps, and the next moment she was alone. She opened the book, which had now become blurred, sniffed hard and began to read. The biographical details were on the inside cover at the front. 'John Cunningham,' she read silently, 'has lived in South America for the past twenty years. A dedicated animal lover and conservationist, he travels the world for material for his books, but always returns to the place he loves, his home in a remote part of Amazonia where he lives with his wife Olivia and an aviary of exotic birds that he has rescued from injury or death. He is also interested in helping to preserve ancient Indian tribes and their customs, and will shortly, he assures us, be writing a book on his experiences.'

She held the book to her, savouring the new discovery of the man who had always been a stranger to her, but soon would be a stranger no longer.

'Dad, oh, Dad,' she whispered. 'If only I'd known before!' Her words carried a sadness, an echo from childhood of something lost and beyond recall. She put the book down, to read it more fully at her leisure later, when she would be alone.

Roarke was standing, and had laid a thick cloth on the table where the typewriter stood. 'Here it is,' he said, 'all ready.'

Joanna sat down at the table and saw the stack of papers waiting to be typed. An empty, open briefcase told its own story. 'There's practically a book here now!' she gasped.

'There's all my work for the past three years there. Don't worry, though, I don't expect you to finish it all tonight,' he said drily.

'You mean you just carry it around with you?'

'I've never got around to having it typed, if that's what you mean.' He gave an eloquent shrug.

'And I don't suppose you've kept a copy of all you've written?'

'No. Are you going to do a carbon for me?'

'It's no more work. I might as well.' She fitted a carbon paper in between two sheets of typing paper and rolled them expertly in to the machine. Roarke gave a low whistle.

'That was professionally done, for a start!'

'It won't be if you're going to stand there watching,' she retorted pertly. But for the very first time she felt a small sense of achievement. She had—as far as he was concerned—actually done something right. Quite absurd, the least important thing, loading a typewriter correctly with paper. Any secretary or typist in the world could have done it the same way, and there would have been nothing surprising in that, but *she* had startled him.

'I can take a hint,' he answered. 'You're as good as alone. I shan't watch.' And he walked away and settled himself down at her recently polished table and began to write.

The next hour passed in total silence as far as conversation was concerned. The metallic rattle of typewriter keys was a constant accompaniment, but Joanna, deeply engrossed, wasn't even aware of time passing until Roarke's voice said: 'Coffee.'

She looked up and flexed her fingers and rubbed her face. 'Oh, thanks. I didn't realise——'

He riffled through the neatly typed sheets that she had stacked at the side of the table. 'You're quick,' he remarked. She was aware that his tone held great surprise. She wouldn't have expected otherwise. 'You're also—as far as I can see—spot on.'

'And considering your writing, that's a miracle,' she said drily.

He drew in his breath sharply between clenched teeth. 'Ouch!'

'I know you think I'm a social butterfly,' she went on. 'But it doesn't mean I'm all cotton wool between the ears. I can, and this may astonish you, read, and write, and count to more than ten—I can also type neatly because if I decide to do anything, I do it well. I hope I make myself clear.' It was a beautifully formed little speech, and the irony of her words was not lost on him. He had used the same final words to her on more than one occasion. She was returning them to him gently and effectively.

It was like a delicate verbal fencing match, and she awaited his riposte with interest. It came. 'The word, I think, is—*touché*,' he answered. 'But did I ever imply that I thought you stupid?'

'No,' she admitted. 'Arrogant, spoiled, conceited, a bitch—they're a few of the words you've used. Not stupid—but you didn't need to. You obviously do—or did—think so. Anyway, I'm only doing what millions of people the world over can do just as well. Don't let the fact that you can't type give you an inferiority complex.' She allowed the briefest pause. 'That was a silly thing to say. You wouldn't, would you? You're pretty superior.' She spaced the last two words out for the fullest effect. And she watched his reaction. It was on again, the battle of wills and words, and she felt alert and alive as never before. She saw an answering spark of something deep in his eyes and knew that she had scored.

His mouth twitched, but he didn't smile. His eyes were deep hard pools of grey in the light. 'As long as you realise that,' he said easily, 'it will make life so much easier for you—while we're stuck here. I know this terrain, you don't. You're as out of your element as a fish out of water. It's the law of the jungle here—literally—and while you may be queen of the social jungle—or whatever you care to call it, that counts for nothing here.' He paused. The air had grown still, the large room a place of heightened awareness as they faced each other across the table, he large and dark and still faintly menacing in his all-black clothes, she smaller, more physically fragile in contrast, yet determined to yield not an inch in the battle.

She laughed, deliberately shattering the tension into a thousand fragments. 'You've a fancy way with words,' she mocked. 'Queen of the jungle? That's good! And who are you? Tarzan?' She rose to her feet. 'You've been going on about something being wrong—*you* have a sixth sense. You go out dressed like a soldier on manoeuvres, carrying a gun—you're like a child, play-acting—I think you're making it all up, do you know that? Just so that you can act the part of the tough hero to impress silly little me.' She banged her hand on the table. 'Well, it doesn't, Mr Tough-Guy Roarke! You amuse me, you really do. And I swallowed it—I really must have been stupid! But I'm not now. I can see through you. I've been typing your notes, don't forget, and I've done enough to see that you're really living in a fantasy world. You've let all those expeditions go to your head. You might cater to wealthy Americans or whatever, who'll pay thousands of dollars to act out their dreams of finding lost Inca cities, or gold treasures, but you're not. catering to *me*. I didn't come here by choice, remember? I came because you damned well hijacked me, and I've had enough of it, do you hear? I'll prove it right now. I'm going outside—and don't try to stop me!' And so saying she marched to the door.

She had reached, and unbolted the front door, and Roarke hadn't come after her. He hadn't said a word during her tirade either. He hadn't, she also realised, looked embarrassed or guilty. He had listened with apparent calm—surprising in one so quick-tempered. She tried to pull open the door, but it wouldn't budge.

She swore and pulled harder, and his voice came: 'It's locked with a key, Joanna.'

'Then, damn you, I'll go out through the cellar!' She turned to face him, eyes sparkling with temper.

'You won't, you know,' he said in a quiet, calm way.

'Want to bet?' she flashed.

'Try it, and see how far you get,' he answered, then a stillness came over him, and he stood there, large, quiet—and somehow, suddenly, and in what way she could not have said, very frightening. She froze, heart beating rapidly. This, now, was like nothing that had gone before. This was real, very real, and he meant what he said. His tone was deadly, and whatever sparks had flown before, whatever tension had gathered, was as nothing compared to what was happening now.

'I won't let you stop me,' she warned him. 'You think you can, but I'll prove to you——'

'I *know* I can stop you, and I will. You are not going out of this house tonight for any reason. It's quite simple.' He folded his arms and leaned negligently against the doorpost. 'So if you're intending to try, carry on. You won't even reach the kitchen door, I promise you.'

He meant it, every word. Yet now, to Joanna, it had become more than a battle of mere words. It had become a deadly challenge, and it was important to her that she did not fail. And it had all been triggered off because Roarke had made a remark about her typing . . .

'I'll go when I'm ready,' she retorted smartly. 'Do you think I'll just march out now and let you bring me back? Hah! You'll have to go to the bathroom some time—I can wait. You'll see!'

He pushed himself away from the door and walked over to her. 'So I will,' he said equably, 'and when I do, *this* is what I'll do with you.' His next movements were so swift and unexpected that she had no time to draw breath. He picked her up, held her helplessly pinned against him and carried her up the stairs.

He pushed her into her room and locked the door while she was still gasping for breath, and walked away, whistling. Joanna hammered at the door, shouting, calling his name—and other names that she hadn't thought of calling him before—when the door was unlocked and opened abruptly in mid-tirade and he pulled her out. 'Downstairs,' he said, not gently, holding her arm—not gently in that either. 'See? Simple, wasn't it? Though why I should waste my time on you, why I don't just let you go, I'll never know. I must be mad.'

'Let go of me, you arrogant beast!' she stormed, and wrenched herself free. 'Don't *touch* me. You're revolting!' She ran down the stairs, furious, and he followed. 'Damn you—*damn* you!' She ran into the drawing room and slammed the door shut and he followed, flinging it open again.

'Do your own bloody typing!' she yelled, and swept the papers to the floor in a grand sweeping gesture.

Roarke stood by the door. 'Pick them up,' he ordered.

'Pick them up yourself,' she retorted.

'I'll ask you once more. Pick up the papers.'

'No!'

'Okay, don't say I didn't give you the choice.'

She was ready for him when he came towards her. Ready, but not quite quick enough. Before she could put her intentions into action she was kneeling on the floor by the table, one hand behind her back, the other free. He applied the merest fraction of pressure and she bit her lip. How foolish she had been to try and defy him she was just beginning to realise. It was obvious that he knew far more tricks than she did and was prepared to use them.

'All right, damn you, let me go. I'll pick them up.'

Instantly she was free, and gritting her teeth she picked up every single sheet of paper. She slammed them on the desk. 'Boy,' she snapped, 'I'll bet you feel really good, using force on a woman! You'd think twice if I was a man.' Her eyes blazed.

'I can't imagine any man throwing the kind of tantrum you do,' was the smooth retort. 'What did you expect me to do? Stand meekly by and then pick up the papers myself? No way, Joanna. If you decide to behave in a fairly civilised manner, we'll get along fine——'

'No, we won't,' she cut in. 'Not in a million years. We'd never manage that. You were prejudiced before you met me——'

'True,' he murmured, and nodded. 'I've not had much cause to change my opinion either. You should have been spanked soundly from childhood onwards. I'll bet you had everything your own way from birth. But you won't get it from me, not as long as we're here together, so just try and remember it, it will make things a lot easier for you.'

'You expect me to be meek and docile?'

'God forbid! I didn't say that, nor would I expect it. What's wrong with manners—and consideration? Have you ever tried either in your life?' His words, quietly said, were devastatingly effective, like hammer blows to her wounded self-esteem, and she caught her breath, for once unable to answer.

Roarke walked away from her and then turned. 'You offered to type for me—I accepted. In the middle of it you began to try and needle me by saying all the dangers were in my imagination—I was play-acting, living in a dream world. I'm going to tell you something now that I didn't want to tell you before, because there was no point in worrying you needlessly. I found the body of an Indian about a mile away, on the banks of the river. The body was headless. Someone had hacked off his head, Joanna, and it wasn't a pretty sight. Do you know what that means?'

Her legs had turned, unaccountably, to indiarubber, and she sat down ashen-faced. 'I'll tell you what it means,' he went on relentlessly. 'It means that somewhere about are headhunters. They're primitive nomadic tribes of savages who do precisely what their name implies—they hunt heads. Their weapons are usually poison-tipped arrows or darts. How do you think they'd look forward to acquiring a beautiful blonde female head?' He walked slowly towards her. 'Have you ever seen a shrunken human head?'

'Yes, once,' she whispered, lips scarcely moving.

'So have I. Pretty, aren't they? The ideal ornament for any home. Do you *know* what they *do* to achieve that shrunken effect?'

She shook her head, fighting off nausea that threatened to overcome her. 'I don't want to to know,' she whispered. She put her hand to her mouth.

'Then I won't tell you. But I brought you here, and I'm responsible for your safety, and I'll stop you from venturing outside the protection of this house even if I have to knock you out and tie you up——'

Joanna heard no more. As she tried to stand, a rushing, roaring sound, as of a giant waterfall, filled her head, drowning her in darkness, and finally, merciful oblivion.

She came round to find herself lying on her bed. Sick and faint, she looked at the man crouched over her, but he was blurred and out of focus. She struggled to sit up and he pushed her back. 'Stay still for a minute,' he cautioned. 'Get your balance back. We're safe here, inside. The house has alarms, and I've activated them. If anyone tries to get in, we'll know in good time.'

He laid his hand on her burning forehead. 'I shocked you deliberately because it was the only way to make you listen. I'm not proud of it, but I had to do it. We're not in Rio—or London—although often places like those are infinitely more dangerous than any jungle. You have only to read the newspapers to be aware of that. But you're used to the cities. You can survive, because you learned how to. Here the laws are totally different. I'd rather walk through a jungle at night than Central Park in New York—but only because I know these places better. I'm at home here, and I'm used to it. You're not.' He still had his hand on her forehead, his touch gentle and alien to his words, which were harsh and hard hitting. 'You'll be safe with me as long as you understand that.'

He sighed. 'Our personal feelings don't enter into it, Joanna. I've been tough on you because that is the only way I know how to be. I shan't change.'

She shivered slightly and he lifted her up so that she was sitting. Then he pushed two pillows at her back to prop her up. 'You're tough too,' he reminded her. 'Don't forget that. For a woman you're exceptionally strong, and you're no coward, but you're not in your own world. This is a different sphere from yours, and always will be.' His dark grey eyes looked into hers, and his hands on her arms were infinitely warm and strong, and he seemed almost unaware that he was holding her.

'You are your father's daughter,' he said softly, and his hands tightened imperceptibly on her arms, and something changed. Like an electric current flowing between them, a heightened perception and awareness that owed nothing to like or dislike, but was beyond it, almost primitive in intensity, something above and way beyond the normal senses.

They became very still, and there was silence after his words, neither of them speaking or moving. Joanna could not have spoken anyway. His words had gone deeply home, the truth of them blinding. He made her see things that no one ever had before—and more, he made her know the truth of them. He was not only tough and powerful, he was also wise. She saw herself clearly through his eyes—vain, shallow, utterly selfish. She did not particularly like herself any more—and wondered for the first time if she had ever.

'Thank you for telling me all this,' she said quietly. 'Do you mind if I stay here for a few minutes?'

'Of course. You're all right?'

'I'm quite all right, thank you.' She looked at him. 'The truth can sometimes be a shock, and you've told me the truth about a lot of things.' The words hung in the air, and there was a stillness, as though time had paused on its way, and their eyes met and held, and something radiated all around them, filling her, filling him, a magic time that didn't belong to the world but was apart from it.

And Roarke knew, for he took his hands away from her arms as though with great difficulty, and she heard his indrawn breath, saw a muscle move in his jaw, and the shimmering threads of tension wrapped round them and enfolded them, and it was something rare and precious. She was sharply conscious of him, of every inch of him, his face imprinted for all time on her mind in a blazing awareness of everything he was.

She longed for him to take her, hold her, her body tingling with sudden warmth at the knowledge—and he stood up and moved away, as if something of that had reached him and he was disturbed.

'Come down when you're ready,' he said, and went out, soft-footed. He moved lightly and quietly for all his size. Joanna shivered. She knew that he was as well aware of some intangible force as she was. She had not imagined the tension that had been in the room before—or his reaction to it.

She recalled their first meeting, the explosive violence

she had sensed beneath the surface of the man then, and she knew it to be very true. It could be transmuted to something else. In love, he would be fiery and with a violence of a different kind. She knew at that moment that she wanted him to make love to her, and felt no shame at the knowledge, only a heightened perception of what he would be like. For an instant, before, it had seemed as though he had been about to kiss her. That too had not been her imagination. She felt as if she could almost read his thoughts.

Joanna lay back, eyes open, gazing at the darkened ceiling but seeing only Roarke's face. There were great dangers outside, but he had sworn to keep her safe, and he would, in spite of her foolish actions. He would have stopped her leaving, she knew that. No one ever before in her life had assumed the role of protector. It was new, rather strange—and it was a good safe feeling to have. She hugged her arms where his hands had held her and rubbed them lightly. Other men had held her, kissed her, tried to make love to her, but none had had the effect that Roarke had merely by touching her. Her senses were aware of him to a degree she had never known, her nerve ends tingling at the memory of his hands upon her arms. She moistened her lips with her tongue, remembering his mouth on hers, briefly, oh, so briefly. She wanted him as she had never wanted a man before. She wondered if, in his wisdom, he knew that too.

She sat up and swung her feet to the floor. It was time to go down. A lot of typing awaited her, and lying there thinking about it wouldn't get it done. Lying there thinking about Roarke making love to her was not doing her any good either. She went to wash her face and hands, combed her hair, then went downstairs.

Everything was beginning to change, subtly and imperceptibly, the balance shifting from what it had been before to something entirely different. Joanna was relieved to have work to do, for life would have been intolerable doing nothing. More than once she glanced up, aware of Roarke's eyes upon her, but when she did, he was apparently engrossed in his writing.

At midnight she stood up. 'I'll make coffee,' she announced.

'Fine. Thanks.' He didn't look up, but his pen was motionless, as if he didn't know what to put next—or as if he waited for her to go before continuing. Joanna was feeling irritable, not knowing why, but tired enough not to want to say anything that might provoke a reaction from him. Edgy, nerves ragged, she spilt some water on the floor and had to mop it up before putting the kettle on. It was the feeling of being penned in that was partly responsible. She had not put her face out of doors for two days, and a pressure seemed to be growing, invisibly weighing down on her—and, she was quite sure, on Roarke as well. Her head ached, and while it could be due to the concentration on typing, she doubted that was the cause, although it was tiring work.

She put her hand to her forehead, longing to have something cool to put on it. She was warm, and her hair was damp with perspiration despite the efficient air-conditioning. She looked round her at the kitchen. The blinds were down over the windows, the doors to outside were locked. She felt stifled and uneasy.

The kettle boiled, and Joanna was about to fill the cups with instant coffee when she froze, listening. A faint noise had come from outside the window, a crackling sound as though of twigs being trodden on—stealthily. She ran out swiftly towards the drawing room. 'Roarke, come quickly,' she said. 'I heard a noise from outside.'

He stood, strode past her and went ahead into the kitchen. Then he switched out the light and stood waiting, listening. She came closely behind him and whispered: 'Outside the window, twigs breaking.' He nodded. Breathlessly she stood there, all her irritation draining away in the immediacy of possible danger. Her skin crawled as she heard the sound repeated, but farther away now, and she caught his arm. The answering pressure of his hand told her that he too had heard. He turned and mouthed in her ear: 'Keep away from the window. I'm going outside.'

'No!' she clung on to his arm with both hands.

'I have to.' He whirled her round and half carried her into the hall, out of earshot of anyone outside the kitchen. 'Stay here. Let me in when I return.'

She stared at him wide-eyed in her dismay, fearful. 'Stay—please, we're safe here—you said so——'

'And I'm not standing around waiting for something to happen. That's not my way, Joanna. I want to get the bastards.'

'What if they get you first?' she asked, tight-lipped.

He gave a wry grin. 'They won't. I've got cat's eyes in the dark. They haven't. In fact I'm surprised there's anyone out. One of them must have been attracted by the lights——'

'You can't guarantee you'll be safe. Supposing there's more than one? And if you don't come back, what then? How long do I wait, for God's sake?'

'If I'm not back by morning, you'll know. Contact your stepmother—the radio frequencies are written down by the transceiver, and tell her to get someone here fast. She'll know what to do. And then——' he paused. 'Just watch out in the market places of Manaos or Rio for a shrunken head that looks like me——' He didn't finish. Joanna struck him hard, anguished, horrified at his flippant, sick joke.

He looked at her. 'Sorry. That wasn't in the best of taste, was it? I asked for that.'

She shivered, suddenly very cold. 'Is that what it is to you? A joke?' she whispered.

'No, I'm deadly serious. It's no joke, but I don't like waiting, I've never liked that. They're murderous savages, and if there are one or two less after tonight, it'll be something.' She was silent at that, remembering his words after his last trip out and how she had seen everything solely from her own viewpoint. Perhaps at last she was really learning. He had to go: it was as simple as that. And, deep inside, she knew that he was right in what he said.

He switched off the alarm by the kitchen door and fastened on his gun-belt, buckling it securely, safely. It seemed a symbolic gesture. No turning back. Joanna's heartbeat was erratic with the fear and tension within her yet she did not speak again, or beg him not to go. She had gone past that stage. He might guess, if she were to, and he must never know the truth about her feelings, for his world was not hers. She had glimpsed his life in the words she was typing; they sprang out from the paper in vivid pictures ready to be imprinted in her mind. She had never thought she could envy anyone in life, for she had everything. She belonged to the golden people, and they were the envy of everyone, everywhere. And yet now she was seeing something infinitely richer in variety than she had ever known, and it was quite disturbing. She was seeing exploration, and wonder, and the joy of discovery—and with humour too, rich veins of laughter running through the pages and mingling in a glorious blend with the more serious matters.

There was no champagne at parties in remote Andean villages, merely a local firewater, and llama milk drunk out of ancient silver to the musical accompaniment of chattering monkeys and shrieking macaws. No caviare and smoked salmon, but llama meat and avocadoes ripe from the trees. It should have been ridiculous, laughable—but it wasn't.

Roarke opened the door. 'Wish me luck.' She followed him down carrying the torch. The passage was cold with the night, and smelt faintly damp. She saw him unbolt the door, and she wasn't going to cry. He half turned, and she smiled.

'Good luck, Roarke. I'll be waiting.' He nodded, already mentally outside, and slipped out like a dark shadow. She bolted the door and leaned on it, eyes dry, throat aching. 'Please God, bring him safely back.' She had not prayed for a long time.

She turned and went back, took typewriter and papers out to the kitchen, and began to type again.

# CHAPTER SIX

THE words had scarcely any meaning, and Joanna typed mechanically without being aware of the content. All the time she was listening, ears attuned to the faintest sound from the cellar. She made the minutes go faster by setting herself a target for each page, and trying to beat it, and ignoring any other considerations. It didn't work, but it helped a little.

At three o'clock in the morning she was fighting exhaustion, struggling to keep awake, but she was making too many mistakes. She put her head down on the table, knowing that she must not fall asleep, but too tired to remain sitting upright.

She heard the taps coming and jerked her head up, not realising for a moment what had roused her. Then, suddenly alert, she ran down the cellar steps and opened the door.

Roarke fell in, nearly knocking her over. She pulled him up as best she could, bolted the door and supported him as he leaned against the rocky passage wall, the blood smears on his face telling a frightening story. 'Come on,' she said, hiding the dreadful fear of what might have happened to him as she put her arms round him to help him. 'Come into the light.'

Their way was slow, but they reached the kitchen and he sat down in her chair, the blood a deep red against the ghastly whiteness of his face. 'Dear lord,' she whispered. 'Roarke—what happened?' She poured him a drink of water and he drank, then looked up at her. A faint grin accompanied his words as he said: 'I had to do something to stop you lecturing me when I came in——'

'For God's sake, Roarke! What happened to you?'

He put his hand to his forehead, removed it, stared at his bloodstained fingers in apparent surprise, and gave a low whistle. 'Hell,' he said, with feeling, 'no wonder you went pale! It looks worse than it is—and no, it is not a wound from a curare-tipped dart, so you can stop looking so concerned. I'm not going to seize up or fall into a fit or——' he stopped, and swayed slightly. Joanna grabbed hold of him and steadied him.

'Don't try and talk,' she said urgently. 'Can you make it to the drawing room?' She looked into his eyes. 'Nod if yes.'

'Mmm,' he said instead, and she took a deep breath and helped him to his feet, he leaning heavily with his arm across her shoulders, and walking slowly. She saw him comfortable on the settee, then knelt by him, searching his scalp to see what kind of wound it was. The blood was clotting now, and she feared to touch, but there was an ugly gash running practically from left ear to temple. It needed cleaning and disinfecting as swiftly as possible. She ran out and fetched clean cloths, bowl of water and bottle of antiseptic solution from the kitchen, and kneeling again beside him, began to clean very delicately around the wound.

'I winged two of them,' he said slowly, after a minute. 'It was too dark to see anything, but I got the bastards because I heard them yell as I ran. I was chasing them when I got the backlash from a branch they'd pushed aside—full smack on to my head. If that hadn't happened, I'd have got them for sure.'

She listened in horror, not daring to say anything but wanting to ask more. Had it been the headhunters outside the house? Worse—were they likely to come back? That was the most urgent question of any.

'I saw stars—literally, for a few seconds and they'd gone.'

'Oh, Roarke, thank God you're all right! It's clean now. I might have to snip off some hair and put a dressing——'

'No, you won't. It's clean. Leave it, let the air get to it. I've had far worse than this.'

'But it needs——'

'No, I'm okay. Don't you understand? You've done your nurse bit for the night—you look like I feel. Get some rest. I'll keep watch——'

'If you think I'm going to rest, you're stupid, or mad, or both,' she said, standing up. 'You're the one who——'

'Shut up! I need a brandy—a big one.'

Tight-lipped, Joanna stalked over to the drinks cupboard and returned with a glass of brandy, which she handed to him. He looked at it, drained it in one go, then looked at her. 'I said a *big* one. B-I-G, big. Not half a bloody teaspoon!'

She snatched the glass from him, had a better idea, handed it back to him, marched over with the bottle and handed that to him. 'Here,' she said, 'pour your own.'

'Thanks, I will.' He poured himself a liberal measure and put the bottle on the floor. 'Have one yourself,' he suggested.

She glared, icy-eyed, at him. 'No, thank you,' she answered stiffly, 'one of us has to keep sober.'

'This won't make me anything like drunk. And don't be so bloody po-faced. I'm not asking for sympathy and I can do without lectures, so don't even start. Your fine intentions didn't last long, did they? You might have well as greeted me with your usual line, "It took you long enough." I'm getting quite used to that.'

'Oh, go to hell!' she retorted. 'There's not much wrong with you. Your tongue's in good working order anyway——'

'So's the rest of me,' he cut in. 'Good grief, haven't you been reading what you've been typing, for God's sake? I was semi-knocked out for a few moments, that's all. I've had far worse, I promise you.' He swallowed some of the brandy and nodded. 'Get my cigars, there's a good girl. On the table.'

Wordlessly she obeyed, and struck a match to light the slim black cheroot, and asked: 'Anything *else*?' in a voice dripping with sarcasm.

He blew a long stream of blue smoke. 'Ah, beautiful! No, thanks. Sit down, rest your legs.'

The man who had staggered—she would have sworn only semi-conscious—not ten minutes previously, dripping blood and as white as a sheet, should have been lying back regaining his strength, not sitting sipping fine old brandy and enjoying a cigar. Joanna would not have believed it possible if she hadn't seen it with her own eyes. He had lost none of his acid-sharp tongue either. Her feelings were mixed. Relief vied with temper, and she wasn't sure which was uppermost. She only knew that he was the most complex, and maddening—and utterly fascinating—human being she had ever encountered.

He sat back comfortably, long legs stretched out the full length of the settee, adjusted a cushion behind him and sighed. 'Ah, that's better!'

Joanna sighed as well, but she wasn't sure why. She might as well ask him the questions she had feared to ask in his apparently delicate state before. If the events of the night hadn't thrown him, nothing else would.

'Roarke,' she began, 'was it the headhunters we heard outside the house?'

'I don't know,' he answered surprisingly. 'I was pretty far away when I spotted them. It could have been an animal searching for food that we heard. I gather that your father isn't averse to throwing out food scraps and then waiting with loaded camera for whatever comes along.'

'Oh. Then that rather cancels out my second question, which was—are they likely to come back?'

'If it was them, what do you think? After being shot at? Would you? Don't forget that to them, guns are magic, white man's magic. They're not to know how many there are of us here—or how many more "flashing lights that spit fire" that we have. We can ride this out if we keep our cool, that's all.'

Joanna jumped to her feet and fetched an ashtray in the nick of time. 'Thanks,' he said. He finished the brandy and his cigar at the same time, then lay back, closing his eyes. 'I do feel absolutely splendid,' he announced. 'I'll keep watch, you have a rest.' The next moment he was fast asleep, breathing deeply and steadily. Joanna crept up to him, removed the empty glass from his hand, and crept away stealthily again. She curled up in an armchair and watched him. His chest rose and fell rhythmically, and she envied the complete relaxation of a man who had been through so much to fall asleep within seconds of closing his eyes.

It was obvious that he wasn't going to wake up for a while. She went up to both bedrooms, removed the covers from the beds and took them down. She covered Roarke first, switched out the lights, leaving one on in the hall, casting a pleasantly dim light, curled up in her armchair with a footstool at her feet, and covered herself. It was reassuring that he had gone to sleep. She had sufficient respect for his instinct to know that he would have stayed awake, alert and sober, had danger been near. She intended, nonetheless, only to rest, not to sleep.

When she awoke it was dawn, and Roarke had gone from the settee. She sat bolt upright, for a moment worried, then heard running water from the distance, and relaxed. He was somewhere upstairs, probably having a shower. She was stiff and sore and aching in every muscle from sleeping in an unaccustomed position. The night had gone, and with it the need to stay down. Taking her cover, she went up the stairs and into her room, flung the cover on the bed then went and knocked at his door.

'Roarke?' she called.

'Come in, it's not locked,' he answered, and she went in.

His bathroom door was ajar, and she could hear water splashing. 'I'm in the shower,' he said. 'Everything okay?'

'Yes. Can I go to bed for a while?'

'Of course. You didn't look very comfortable in the chair.'

'I wasn't,' she shouted. 'I'm aching all over—not complaining, you understand, but achi——' her voice faded away as he walked in, rubbing his hair with great care. He was dressed only in a towel that he had tied round his waist. She swallowed. 'Aching,' she finished. He was quite something, stripped. And Joanna had seen practically all there was to see in male physiques, on the various yacht decks and beaches of the world's resorts. But this was something else.

He very probably knew it; she couldn't be sure because he didn't have the air that most men with superb bodies do, the 'look at me, aren't I the greatest?' kind of conceit that oozes out and is obvious to all. His shoulders were broad, powerful, and as heavily muscled as his arms and legs. Not the ugly muscle of the professional body-builder, but the working muscles of a very powerful man indeed. Dark hair, not too thick, but interestingly sexy, covered his chest, arms and legs, and his tan was deep, a fact she already knew. He finished rubbing his hair and began drying his arms. 'Sorry,' he said, no trace of regret in his voice, 'you should have said, I'd have had the chair.'

'You fell asleep the moment you finished your brandy,' she retorted. 'I wouldn't have dreamed of waking you.' But she didn't want to stay. He was having the most disturbing effect on her. It was difficult to concentrate on what she was saying.

'Did I?' he looked vaguely blank. 'I don't remember.'

'No,' she began to back towards the door. 'Well, I must be going——'

'There's no need to run out like a frightened virgin,' he said. 'Don't tell me my semi-nakedness upsets you?' There was the faintest gleam of mockery in his dark eyes, and a faint smile to his mouth.

She laughed. How she managed to do it she didn't know, but it sounded genuine. 'Good grief,' she answered, 'do I look scared?' She gave him a cool assessing look from top to toe, and then back again. She yawned daintily. 'I'm tired, that's all. How's your head?'

'You'd better check. I've been careful not to touch.' And he walked towards her, leaving a trail of damp footprints on the floor. Joanna wished she hadn't asked now. He inclined his head for her inspection, and she could smell the clean damp soapy smell of him, and wished she hadn't come up. Her heart pounded so hard that she feared he would hear it.

'I—er——' it came out as a squeak, so she cleared her throat and tried again. 'I think it's healing nicely. Yes, so it is.' She had reached up carefully to part the thick hair surrounding the gash. 'Er—I'll clean it again just to make sure if you like.' Her voice wobbled ever so slightly. She hoped that he hadn't noticed.

'I really do believe you're nervous, Miss Joanna,' he

mocked, and he was, for some perverse reason of his own, enjoying the situation. 'Very interesting!'

'Don't talk rubbish,' she shot back. 'I'm—I'm——' She froze in terror as he slid his arms around her. 'What are you doing?' she breathed.

His eyes were dark upon her. 'You looked as if you were going to fall,' he answered, which was a lie. He was teasing her and she didn't like it because although at any other time she would have responded flippantly and quite confidently, now, for some absurd reason, she couldn't. She felt like a gauche schoolgirl, a new experience.

'Well, I'm not,' she retorted, 'so you can let me go——' and she moved smartly to be free. Roarke let her go, which, perversely, annoyed her.

'My mistake,' he said gravely. 'Off you go like a good girl, and fetch the antiseptic. I'll try and be more decently clad when you come back.'

'Hah! It wouldn't bother me if you weren't,' she retorted, and went out.

He was sitting on the bed when she returned a few minutes later, and was dressed in jeans. 'Hold that,' she ordered, giving him the bowl of warm water. She stood in front of him and cleaned the wounded area with antiseptic-soaked cotton wool while he sat motionless and impassive.

'There, done,' she announced. 'Healing nicely. There's a long scab. Try not to touch it—and don't comb your hair.'

'Will you, then?'

She sighed. 'I suppose so. Where's your comb?'

'On the dressing table.' She fetched it and said:

'Lift up your head a bit.' He obeyed. Joanna hid a grin at that. She couldn't imagine that he would be used to obeying orders. She found great pleasure in combing his hair, which, although still damp from washing, was drying. He had closed his eyes when she began, and she took her time, suddenly aware that it was having an effect on him. There was a faint smile on his lips, and he made a little sound in his throat at one point, so that she cried: 'Did I hurt you?'

He opened his eyes, and they were unfocussed for a moment. 'What?' he said, as if he had been miles away, voice blurred.

'I thought I'd hurt you,' she soothed, suspicions confirmed. He needed paying back for having mocked her when he had been clad only in a towel, and she knew just the way to do it. 'You shouldn't leave your hair wet, you know, not with that nasty gash.' She lifted his abandoned towel from the chair. 'Sit still, I'll rub your head dry and then comb it properly.' She pulled up the chair and sat in front of him. 'Bend your head slightly forward. *That's* it!' Her voice was soothing and encouraging—but inside she was laughing. She knew well from past experience that head massage, hair brushing and combing could be a remarkably sensuous experience. It could be an interesting experiment. Roarke would think twice before he tried to confuse her again when he was underclad!

She started with the towel and then abandoned it, casting it aside. He didn't seem to notice, but she murmured by way of explanation: 'This is finger drying. All the best hairdressers do it occasionally——' he wasn't listening. Eyes closed, head bowed, he was a docile subject for anything she chose to do.

She rubbed his scalp, slowly, fingers massaging with an instinctive skill which surprised even Joanna herself, and he sat utterly relaxed, hands loosely clasped, shoulders slumped forward. She smoothed and soothed, and if he had been lying down he would have been asleep. He was nearly, even so. Fingers stroking, moving round to the back, and forwards again, always scrupulously careful to avoid the scab, back again, to his neck where she stroked upwards with a featherlight touch that was no more than a whisper at the sides of his head, a place very sensitive to touch. He was breathing deeply and steadily, and she paused suddenly, and waited.

After a few moments he opened his eyes. 'Is it finished?' he asked, and he was confused, that was obvious; the words were slurred.

'Not quite,' she answered. 'Are you enjoying it?'

'I—think so,' he murmured.

'Then lie down—on your stomach. Your hair's very thick at the back and I can't reach it properly like this.' He turned round without a word and lay face down, arms outspread, and Joanna knelt beside him and began again. There was only one snag, that she hadn't quite bargained for; she was also becoming affected by what she was doing.

His head was turned slightly aside so that he could breathe. His voice came muffled, almost indistinguishable, and she bent closer to hear. 'Sorry? What did you say?'

'Is this supposed to send me to sleep? It's having the strangest effect,' he mumbled.

'Could do,' she whispered. 'So relax. It won't hurt you if you do. Just—relax, Roarke.'

'Mmm,' he responded.

She stroked the back of his neck slowly, round and round then up, then round again, and—the temptation was totally irresistible—and then she allowed her hands to slide down slightly to his shoulder blades. He started to mumble something, gave up half way, and relapsed again. She did have a perfectly beautiful answer for him if he did query her change of area. She would, if necessary, explain that it was merely her humble effort to repay his valiant defence at repelling various head-hunters. She didn't think, however, that he was about to question anything she chose to do.

To have a man such as he was almost completely in her power was a delightfully heady sensation, fully appreciated by Joanna. He was pliant, completely relaxed, almost—vulnerable. Her knees ached with kneeling and she eased herself into a sitting position beside him, slightly on one hip. Using her right hand only, she began to rub all over his back and shoulders and upper arms. She had never done this before for anyone, and she was fascinated by the smooth hardness of his skin. His shoulders especially were hard, even with his muscles completely relaxed as they were. There was no doubt of the potential power beneath that skin. She didn't want to finish, even though she was tired herself, and her arm ached.

She slithered down until she was lying beside him, her head resting on his outflung arm. This eased the pressure on her, and she began to stroke his back. Fine hairs covered it, not dark, but almost invisible, and something she didn't care to have to explain was most definitely happening to her. She stopped for a rest, leaving her aching hand lying still, and he made no sound, not even a murmur. He was asleep.

Joanna closed her eyes for a moment to allow her rapidly beating pulses to slow, and began to drift helplessly away. She didn't fight it. She would relax for now, and then, in a few minutes, go. She wasn't sure what she had achieved. It was quite clear that it had all been a new experience for Roarke—yet he was quite obviously a sensually experienced man. Thoughts swirled, and his nearness was drugging her senses, and she imagined how he would be, in the act of love—she caught her breath. Such thoughts were dangerous. Her emotions were already confused, tiredness from physical effort mingling with the sheer pleasure and delight of touching his body, and it was a heady mixture . . .

She floated, uncaring, content to lie beside him however briefly, and certainly innocently, and her body was warm from his nearness, the heat of him reaching her, touching her full length. It really was time to go . . .

She opened her eyes, to see that he had opened his and was looking at her.

'You stopped,' he murmured reproachfully.

'You were sleeping——' her eyes widened as she realised just where she was. 'I think I've been asleep too!'

He laughed softly and drew her to him, moving off his stomach and on to his side as he did so. 'You mean we've slept together?' His mouth quirked.

'Yes—no—you'd better rephrase that,' she said shakily.

He kissed her very softly. 'That was marvellous,' he said. 'The massage, I mean, not the sleeping together, which I didn't fully appreciate because I was sleeping, you understand—only I thought you were combing my hair?'

'You were exhausted. It was just to relax you,' she answered, only she wanted him to kiss her again, and she knew that was a reckless idea, but it didn't seem to matter. Something else mattered far more, but she wasn't quite sure how it had happened.

'It did that,' he agreed—and what happened then was as inevitable as time itself. His lips came down on hers in a heady, sweet-tasting kiss that seemed to last no time, or forever, she could not be sure. 'It also did something else to me,' he murmured, and his hand went to her breast and gently rested there, almost as if of its own volition. His eyes had gone very dark now, his mouth very serious. 'Please go, Joanna.'

She stirred faintly, her body aroused to a fever pitch by his touch, and moved herself gently beneath his questing hand, heady with the touch of him. All she knew was that she wanted him. She wanted him more than she wanted anything, she wanted him to take her, hold her, possess her, and make love to her. She knew, belatedly, what had been her true inner reasons for touching him at all. She knew, and she was not ashamed or guilty about it, and she put her hand to his neck and began to massage it gently all over again. 'Make me go,' she whispered.

'I can't do that, and you know it.' They both spoke in low whispers, the mood as fragile as spun glass, ready to be shattered with one discordant note.

'You can do anything you want,' she mocked. 'You told me so.'

'But not that, because you know that I want to make love to you, don't you?'

'Do you?' Her eyes were wide, pupils dilated, her heartbeats threatening to suffocate her. 'How——' she stroked gently, 'do I know that?'

Roarke undid the buttons of her blouse slowly without answering her, then took it off. She could feel his heart pounding when she touched his chest, then she took his hand and held it to her breast. He was breathing rapidly and shallowly now, his eyes upon her nearly black with desire. He swallowed hard. 'For God's sake,' he said thickly, 'Joanna, I can't help——'

She moved sensuously nearer to him and kissed him, effectively silencing him as their burning lips met. His lips explored the sweetness of her mouth and she bit the lower one gently, teasingly, and he cried out something, some word of anguish, and she laughed and moved slightly away, revelling in his eyes on her body. Hungry, desperate eyes.

Slowly, inexorably, his head came down to her breasts, and he closed his eyes, while she held him closely to her, her heart bursting with love, her body aching with her need for him.

Then there were no more words, all was touch and sensation, and great and wonderful urgency—and when she thought that she would go mad, Roarke took her in a sweeping, tempestuous wave of mounting passion that escalated to a wildness she had never thought possible.

He led her far beyond anywhere she had ever known, took her to the dizzy heights of fulfilment and beyond, to a heart-stopping, earth-shaking climax . . .

She lay still, aching and bruised, utterly sated, and could not speak or move for a long time. Roarke touched her face. 'Joanna?' he said.

She turned her head slowly. 'Yes?'

'Are you all right?'

She took a deep breath. 'No. But I don't want to feel any other way. If I die now, it will be the right moment. I've known everything.'

He laughed softly. 'That was just the beginning,' he said softly.

Her breathing was gradually returning to normal. 'You mean—there's more—than *that*?'

'Much more. Much, much more.' He lay back. 'I'll go and get us a drink in a minute.' He closed his eyes, and moments later, inevitably, was asleep. No wonder, Joanna thought.

She went down after a while and made two cups of coffee. When she returned with them she slid into the bed beside him and woke him up. 'Coffee,' she murmured. '*I* made it.'

'Mmm, sorry. Was I asleep?'

'Yes, you were.'

'Then you can blame your massage for that.'

'Among other things,' she said quietly. She was still recovering. She needed that coffee—oh, how she needed it!

Roarke drank his, took her half empty cup from her and put it away from the bed, then pulled her down.

'Where were we?' he said huskily.

'Roarke, please—not——' But his mouth silenced her, and his hands took her again, skilfully, expertly, and she realised, after only moments, that he was even more aroused than he had been before—which didn't seem to be possible, but proved to be so.

This time there was no urgency, no desperate haste, only a gentle leisurely possession and taking that was infinitely more powerful for it being so. He led her then along paths she had never imagined in her wildest fantasies, their bodies ablaze with heat and a fire that swept them along to ecstasy, and ultimately, a perfect fulfilment . . .

They lay locked in each other's arms and slept for a long while afterwards.

The reaction to what had happened set in later. Joanna hadn't expected it to be so, and she was in the kitchen making a belated meal when it swept over her. She paused in the middle of stirring the soup that she was heating, and she was horrified at herself. She had behaved wantonly, totally wantonly—she had practically seduced Roarke—and she had done so deliberately. She had never before cared what anyone thought about her, going her reckless, pleasure-seeking way with no thought to anyone's opinions, but this was different. Roarke, too, had changed since their lovemaking frenzy. He was quieter, almost subdued, and she suddenly knew, with the insight she had to his inner thoughts, that he regretted what had happened. Nothing had been said about it. It was like an episode that was to be kept separate from their everyday activities; a different time, a different place, apart.

She had slept, and when she had awoken he was not there. She had showered and dressed and gone down to find him busily writing in the drawing room. Something had been not quite right then, but she had put it down to her imagination. Roarke had been polite, courteous, considerate, asking her how she was—but there had been a dreadful barrier. And in the hours since, when she had typed, he had vanished for a long time. The work had been sufficiently engrossing for her not to have to think about him, but when at last he had come back, to tell her that he had seen to the birds in the aviary, and contacted Rio by radio, it was in a remote, impersonal way, far different, and in a way worse than their first arrival at the house.

Joanna poured out the soup, cut newly thawed out bread from the freezer, and called him. She observed him carefully, seeking signs that would confirm her fears, and soon had no doubt.

He sat down. 'Thanks.' He seemed preoccupied. Joanna waited until they had both finished eating before she spoke.

'All right,' she said, 'I can see the wall—and I think I can guess why. Shall we just say that we both regret what happened? I'm not imagining that your behaviour has been different ever since—since this morning, but what's done is done. We can't alter anything.'

He looked up, and a muscle moved in his dark shadowed cheek. He needed a shave, and he looked tired. 'You speak very bluntly,' he said.

'I've never been a person to avoid unpleasant issues,' she answered. 'I don't think you are, either.'

'No, I'm not. I should never—have——' he hesitated, 'made love to you, but,—as you say, what's done is done.'

'And it was, after all, my fault,' she said softly.

'I didn't say that.' His voice was hard and harsh.

'You didn't need to.' She gave a bitter smile. 'I'm well aware that I "seduced" you—for want of a better word.'

'Don't be bloody stupid,' he said angrily. 'Is that what you've been agonising over? Don't. I wouldn't make love to any woman if I didn't want to, no matter what she did. I desired you, I made love to you. It's quite simple.'

'Well, if it helps, I feel sick with myself,' she said, and stood up. 'I'm sorry, I shouldn't be talking like this— I——' she stopped.

'For God's sake, don't you know *why* I feel so bad?' He banged the table so hard that the plates jumped. 'You came here under *my* protection.'

'We're not living in Victorian times,' she retorted. 'Okay, so it was purely physical. We were together, and Mother Nature took over and before you know it——' she stopped and bit her lip. 'Damn. Oh damn, damn, damn!'

Roarke sighed heavily. 'Let's forget it shall we? Let's pretend it never happened.'

He could probably do that. He had undoubtedly made love to so many women that he had lost count. Joanna hid a wry smile at the irony of it. She had made love to the man she loved and she would never forget it as long as she lived. Once the immediate pangs of remorse faded, she would have full, rich memories. Roarke had simply assuaged a physical need, a bodily hunger that to him was as natural as breathing.

'Sure,' she agreed. 'We will. And don't worry—if it's worrying you, I won't tell my father anything.' She looked at him, and surprised an expression of deep pain on his face. Then she knew.

# CHAPTER SEVEN

JOANNA caught her breath. That aspect of the situation had simply not occurred to her—most possibly because her father was, to her, still an unknown quantity.

'That is what I most deeply regret,' said Roarke.

'Well, don't. As you say, let's forget, shall we? We have other things to think about now. Do they know when they'll arrive?'

'He's made a fast recovery. The day after tomorrow, Friday.'

'Then there's work to be done. Cleaning the house, for a start.' She laughed. 'That should do me good! And before you say it—no, I haven't much idea, but I'll learn.' She too could—had to—make a fast recovery.

The sense of shame and remorse was passing, helped undoubtedly by their airing of it, but more so because of something to look forward to. She even felt, in the midst of her love for Roarke, a pang of sympathy for him. He was tough, hard, aggressive—all these—as she had so recently discovered even more fully. He was also only human. He had made a promise, and broken it. She smiled at his expression. 'You'd be surprised,' she said lightly, 'how well I can adapt to new kinds of work.'

'I believe you. Your typing is a constant source of surprise, for a start. No——' he held up his hand quickly, 'I don't mean that in any derogatory sense—but even experienced typists can make lots of mistakes. You don't, and you're not——' he seemed to hesitate before he said the next word, 'experienced.'

'I'm enjoying it,' she said quickly, wondering if she

was going to read a double meaning into everything he said. 'I've got the hang of your writing now. You must get it typed properly after you leave, all of it, I mean, and send it to a publisher.' She hoped she wasn't babbling.

'I'm going to. Do you want to do more now?'

'I'll type all I can today, then leave it. Tomorrow—house cleaning.'

'I'll help,' he said drily. 'Or did you think I was a male chauvinist pig?'

Joanna smiled, but said nothing in answer to that. 'That will be nice,' she agreed. 'Tomorrow, then. For the moment, however, my typewriter awaits.'

She stood by the drawing room window later as night fell, taking a break from her labours, sipping cold orange juice. Roarke was absorbed in his notes, checking photographs, crossing out, rewriting, generally engrossed. He had the rare ability to concentrate exclusively on what he was doing and switch off from outside distractions, and she regarded him briefly before sitting down again. Head bent, in profile he was interesting to look at, lean and powerful, strong—and tender. She swallowed hard at that and turned away, bumping her desk and sending all the papers flying. 'Oh, damn!' she exclaimed, and knelt to pick them all up. 'Oh, look!' she wailed, as he stood up. 'They're all over the place!'

'Let me help.' He crouched on his haunches beside her and began picking up the various numbered sheets of typing paper while Joanna concentrated on the handwritten ones. It was soon done, and they exchanged heaps, he to put his own less decipherable papers in numerical order, she to check that none of her typing had escaped.

She gave a sigh. 'Done! Not as bad as it looked, after all. Thanks, Roarke.'

'No bother. Sure you're not tired? I only expect you to do what you want to do.'

'I can't sit around, I haven't been out—I need to use my energy somehow——' She stopped, aware of what she had said, and added hurriedly: 'I'm actually enjoying typing, which has rather amazed me. I might find I enjoy cleaning house too. Then I'll get really worried!' She said it very lightly, and he smiled.

Undercurrents were there all the time, she was well aware of that fact. She didn't doubt that Roarke was too, but it was very important now that all their conversations were kept on a light level. That way they could at least exist in some kind of harmony for the next two days. Harmony might not be the right word, she decided. Truce would be more appropriate. Only two or three more days and he would go. He had commitments, people waiting for him. He had work to do. Joanna sat down at her table and he left to go back to his.

And what will I do? she thought. After I've met my father, have stayed and talked for a few more days—and I'm beginning to suspect exactly why he had me brought here—then I'll leave. I'll see him again, of course. We won't ever lose touch, I know that, but where will I go?

She sat staring ahead of her looking blankly into the wall. The curtains at the window were drawn and it was now dark outside, and it seemed as if the way ahead stretched equally darkly. There was Monte Carlo in a month. An invitation from the Goldbergs—friends of her mother's—for a cruise aboard their yacht, *L'Hirondelle*, with nine or ten others, mostly Americans. The yacht was the last word in sumptuous accommodation, with a French chef whose cuisine was famous the length and breadth of the Riviera, and invitations were eagerly sought after, and highly prized, like trophies. After that, in May, a fortnight in Tunisia at the villa of the Orsinis, and in June a house-party in Wimbledon to coincide with the tennis—followed almost immediately by a flying trip to Paris to visit yet more friends in her social circle. It really was quite enough, on reflection, to take her mind off the present situation. Joanna took a deep breath. More than enough, really. By August Roarke would have become just a memory. An interesting one, no getting away from *that*—but everything would be in perspective again, thank goodness.

Or would it? She already knew the answer, could see, from the distance of time and space, the crushing loneliness of her whole existence. Shallow laughter, brittle small talk, rivalry and bitching, spinning round in a candyfloss cocoon of emptiness and hollow emotions, prettily packaged—but with nothing inside. She was at a low ebb, the lowest she had ever been, and she pretended to study the notes in front of her in case Roarke wondered why she was not typing. They blurred and danced, but she persisted, reading without really seeing, her heart heavy with a terrible sadness. She wanted to put her head down on the desk and weep, but if she did that he might want to know why, and that would never do.

White-faced, she read on, sitting very still except to turn the papers over. Her head ached and she burned all over and wondered almost disinterestedly if she were running a temperature. There was a tremor in her hands, but she couldn't do anything about that.

'Want a coffee?' His voice made her start. She shook her head, not trusting herself to answer.

'No? Was that "no"?'

She cleared her throat. 'No, thanks,' but it still came out a croak.

'Joanna?' His voice came nearer, and she stiffened. 'Is there something wrong?' He was beside the table, bending down, a puzzled man.

She shook her head and he put his hand on her chin and forced her to look up at him. She heard his indrawn breath, and she stared at him, tears welling in her eyes, tears of weakness and pain and a thousand other things no one would ever understand. 'Don't you feel well?'

'No,' she croaked. It was true. She felt dreadful.

He put his hand on her forehead. 'Hmm, hot. Have you got a headache? A pain anywhere?'

'A headache—I ache all over—I'll be all right, just leave me.'

'You won't, and I won't. Go upstairs, have a cool shower, then get into bed. I'll bring you something up. You've had all your shots?'

'Yes. It's not that—it's——' but she didn't know, herself.

'Is it something you don't want to talk about—woman's talk?'

'No.' She shook her head. 'Just leave me——'

'Don't be stupid. Go up now. Can you manage?'

'Yes.' She stood up and the room spun frighteningly round, but she put her hand on the desk, and it steadied. He saw, he knew.

'Come on.' He took her arm and led her up the stairs to her room. 'A very quick shower to cool you, and then into bed.'

She walked away from him and into her tiny bathroom. Afterwards, she crawled into bed and lay down. The room was making interesting swaying motions which she didn't fully appreciate, so she closed her eyes.

'Drink this.' His voice roused her and she took a cupful of bitter-smelling liquid from him, and sniffed it.

'Ugh! What is it?'

'Something to make you better. It doesn't taste nice, but the best medicine rarely does.' He watched her drink it, pulling a face as she did so, then smiled. 'You can lie down again.' He had brought a cold damp flannel and laid it on her forehead and held her wrist lightly, looking at his watch as he did so.

'Are you——' she began.

'Ssh!' He looked up after a minute. 'Your pulse is fast, but nothing out of the ordinary. Relax, I'll look after you.'

'But I'm——'

'Ssh, don't talk! Doctor's orders. You've a touch of fever, but you'll live. You're a strong girl. You're going to go to sleep in a few minutes and I'm going to stay here with you, okay?' His face was quite as hard as she had ever known it, but he didn't hate her, he had said so. He hated headhunters and there were several downstairs, waiting for supper, only she wondered why he should have invited them. It seemed important to know.

'Why did you ask them here?' she asked, bewildered.

'Who, Joanna?'

'The—you know—*them*—the——' she lowered her voice to a whisper, 'the headhunters.'

'Ah! They're not—they've gone.'

'But I *saw* them!' She wanted him to understand. Why didn't he understand? She gripped his arm and shook it. 'You let them in the kitchen——'

'Joanna, I promise you they're not here any more. Whatever you saw, they are not here now. Do you want me to go down and look?'

'Oh, no, be careful——' but she couldn't think properly any more. He was getting blurred, and receding alarmingly, then returning. She closed her eyes and was whirled away into sweet oblivion.

When she opened her eyes she was very thirsty, and she didn't know where she was. She struggled to sit up, and immediately a voice came. 'Be careful, Joanna.'

'I'm—in bed!' she announced.

'Yes. How are you?' Roarke came forward and laid

his hand on her forehead. 'Good. Much cooler. You've had a touch of fever, but you've slept for three hours.'

'I don't remember much, except feeling dizzy,' she confessed. 'I'm sorry. I'm never ill.'

He sat down on the bed. Roarke, the big patient man who didn't seem to be in any hurry at all. 'You're not ill now, and you'll be fine after a good night's sleep, okay?'

'If you say so.' She managed a weak smile.

'I do say so. I've brought you some more of that disgusting brew.'

'Yuk! I suppose you expect me to drink it?' She remembered *that*.

'It would help,' he agreed drily. 'It's a herbal mixture—I won't bore you with the contents, but your father swears by it—and he should know, he's lived here long enough.'

She took a deep breath. 'All right, you win. Pass it over, please.'

She took the cup from him. This time she would not flinch. She drank it slowly as though it were sherry or some other pleasant drink, smiled, and handed him the empty cup. 'Thank you.'

A brief flicker of amusement crossed his features. 'Well done,' he said softly. 'You *are* better.'

'A little,' she agreed, then shivered, belying her optimism. She lay back, still tired. 'Am I allowed to eat? I'm rather hungry.'

'Of course. Something hot or cold?'

'Hot. Anything, I'll leave it to you.'

'You're taking a chance!' He stood up. 'Shout if you need me.' And he went out. Joanna lay back feeling much better. She was seeing another side to this man that she loved; a kind, caring side. It didn't quite match the many images she already carried of him in her heart, but when she got used to it, it probably would. She felt safe and warm and protected—and cared for.

She heard his steps on the stairs several minutes later and he came in with a laden tray. He helped her up, propped the pillows behind her, and set the tray on her knees. She peeped at the dishes in pleasant—and hungry—anticipation. She was not disappointed. A gently spiced curry—judging from the aroma—nestled in a bed of rice on one plate, and on the second was a portion of fluffy pink mousse. 'My word,' she exclaimed, 'this looks nice!'

'*Bon appetit,*' he answered. 'I'll leave you in peace while I have mine. I'll come back for the tray when you've done. Can you manage?'

'Yes, fine, thanks.' She tucked in with relish when he had gone, finished both plateful, and lay back replete.

When Roarke returned he was carrying two mugs of coffee. He handed her one. 'I'll be sleeping on the settee again tonight,' he told her. 'Leave your door open. If you call, I'll hear you, don't worry. And in the morning we'll see how fit you are for housework. If you're not, I'll have to do it alone, won't I?'

'And can I watch?'

'If you're good, I might let you.' He smiled. He hadn't often given her a smile like that. He was devastatingly attractive, with good strong white teeth, wide mouth, eyes crinkling into laughter lines.

'Then I'll be good.' She had finished her coffee. He took the beaker and the tray.

'Go to sleep now. Remember, call me if you want anything,' he said.

'I'll remember. Goodnight, Roarke.'

'Goodnight. Sleep well.' He paused on the way to the door, looked at her, then went quietly out.

Joanna snuggled down into her pillows and gradually drifted off into a doze. She awoke some time later to go to the bathroom, got back into bed again and settled down. She felt pleasantly lightheaded, as though tipsy, but much better than she had before. She heard quiet steps from downstairs, the faint creak of a stair, then Roarke entered. Her eyes were half closed, and she watched him walk silently over to the bed, look at her, and then go out.

She slept fitfully, and was aware several times of the shadowy figure coming in, looking at her, then leaving as silently as that first time. As she drifted off finally into deeper sleep it was with a warm glow of awareness that he was keeping sentinel over her. She dreamed only of pleasant uncomplicated things, no more nightmares.

In the morning she was much better. Roarke came in, took a look at her, felt her forehead and her pulse, and told her that she wasn't fit for any work, but could watch him.

'I feel fine,' she protested.

'Perhaps you do—now. But you'll be weak when you get up. You had quite a temperature last night, and you were delirious at one stage.'

'Rubbish! Me, delirious? You're joking!'

'I'm not. You thought the headhunters were having tea downstairs.' A vague memory surfaced for an instant, then was gone.

'Oh,' she said.

'Oh, indeed. And your pulse was like a sledge-hammer—I didn't tell you that either. You can wash and dress and then come down, but you'll sit in the drawing room and sit quietly, you understand?'

She shrugged. 'Okay, if you say so.'

'I do say so.' He sat on the bed. 'It's nearly nine. Want to get up now?'

'If you're starting work. I wouldn't miss that for anything.'

'Then up you get. I'll watch you into the bathroom—and you're to leave the door unlocked.'

Joanna swung her feet over the side of the bed and stood up. Roarke grabbed hold of her as she swayed, and she clung to him.

'Oh, this is silly,' she whispered. 'What's the matter——'

'Nothing—except that you're as weak as a kitten. Come on, let me help you. I'll run your shower for you.' He guided her across the bedroom and into the bathroom which scarcely had room for two to move. He reached across, turned on the water, adjusted the control until it came out lukewarm, and said: 'Are you sure you can manage?'

'Yes!' Mild panic made her breathless.

He smiled faintly. 'You're safe. Safer than you'll ever know, Joanna. But be realistic. You're in no state to look after yourself. Get your nightdress off.'

'No—I——' she protested weakly, and tried to push his supporting hand from her arm.

He spoke harshly, surprising her, causing tears to spring to her eyes. 'For God's sake, Joanna! You could fall and crack your head open on the tiles and then where would we be? Be sensible. I'll close my eyes if you want. But you are *not* going to have a shower alone in your condition.'

She swallowed hard and lifted her arms. 'All right.' He eased her nightdress over her head and held her arm in a strong grip as she stepped under the shower. If he had not held her as he did, she would have fallen, she realised that. The water was a shock to her tender skin, and took her breath awat. Roarke handed her a flannel and she dabbed ineffectually at her arms and shoulders, eyes closed to protect them from the warm jets of water that gushed over her.

'Come here,' she heard his exasperated voice, and the flannel was taken from her. The next moment he was washing her, much as she imagined a nurse would, with a swift impersonal touch that lingered nowhere. 'Right, out you get.' She opened her eyes as she stepped out, to be covered by him in a large towel. He leaned across her and switched the water off. Then he led her into the bedroom, as unresisting and docile as a young child.

She stood, shivering slightly as he rubbed her all over with the huge pink towel. She had never imagined, after the previous day's disastrous incidents, that she would allow him to touch her again. She was not only doing so, but she felt no doubts about the rightness of it. He had finished, and he pushed her to the bed and sat her down. 'Now, clothes,' he told her. 'Anything?'

'Yes. I've washed everything up to date. Drawers and wardrobe.' She sat back, allowing his ministrations to flow around her.

'Legs up,' he instructed briskly, and Joanna obediently lifted her feet from the floor. She began to giggle helplessly, and hiccuped.

'I can manage those, thank you,' she said, and eased her pants on. He handed her a white blouse and flowered skirt, made her stand, and dressed her in them.

'Thank you,' she said softly, and looked at him. He gave a wry grin that held a world of things unspoken, and bowed slightly.

'All ready,' he announced. 'Down for breakfast and a leisurely day.' He took her arm and they went downstairs. She was clean, cool, rested—and being remarkably well cared for. It wouldn't last, of course. She would see to that. She was, after all, feeling much better. But there was something very pleasant about it at the moment, and further than that she didn't choose to analyse.

The morning passed. Roarke was a whizz at housework, and she told him so at one point, and he laughed. He had gone through the drawing room like a super-efficient, super-fast robot, dusting, polishing, vacuuming, cleaning windows, all with maximum results and no wasted effort.

'Ever thought of taking it up?' she teased mildly as he stopped for a cold drink.

'Professionally? *There's* a thought. It would make a change from hacking through jungles with a machete. Yes, I do feel a certain flair for wielding a duster.' He grinned at her. 'Come on, bring your drink. Want to see me assault the kitchen?'

'Love to.' He took her glass from her and followed her out, made her sit in a corner, and began his attack of the large kitchen. Joanna watched him work, and he was a powerhouse of energy, almost crackling with it. The atmosphere, conversely, was one of relaxed harmony. She knew why. She was still weak with the aftermath of a fever. And for that reason his aggression was in abeyance. It made her see yet another aspect of him, one that revealed much of his character, although she was sure he would not be consciously aware of it. But Joanna was. He had the mark of true power and strength; the ability to be gentle. She tucked her feet beneath her chair as he cleaned the floor around her, then he picked her up bodily, chair as well, and set her down in another spot as he finished the place where she had been.

'I wish you'd warned me!' she gasped, and he laughed.

'When I do a job, I do it properly. Think I could have lived with myself if I'd left a dirty patch? Shame on you!'

She began to laugh, then suddenly it turned to weeping—and she knew it with horror and dismay, and couldn't do a thing about it. Tears flooded out, and the more she fought to control them the worse they became.

Roarke lifted her from her chair and held her. 'What

is it? Was it me lifting you?'

'No—no, of course not——' her voice came out muffled and distorted. 'I—don't know what's the matter——'

'Oh, love, don't, don't. You'll make yourself ill again. It's all right, Joanna——' he held her closely to him, soothing, comforting, and she sensed his concern even in the midst of her own distress.

The weeping became a tremulous sobbing which gradually died down, leaving her empty and shaken. He picked her up and carried her into the drawing room, put her on the settee, and sat beside her.

'Now, what happened?' he asked.

She looked at him, dreadfully ashamed of her weakness. 'Oh, Roarke, I'm sorry. I don't know. I started to laugh—then suddenly——' she stopped. 'I just don't know.' But strangely, she was beginning to, only it was nothing she could tell him or anybody—she wasn't even sure if she cared to admit it to herself.

'You're just a poor mixed up girl, aren't you?'

She tried to smile. How near he was to the truth, he would never know. 'That's me,' she answered lightly. 'You must have had more than enough of me. Tell you what, let me make up for it. I'll make us a cup of coffee.'

'Really? Sounds a fair exchange.' He was sitting very near, his dark eyes looking steadily into hers. 'But there's no hurry. Let the floor dry properly. After we've drunk it I'll go and do upstairs. You will stay here and read. Then I'm finished, thank the lord, and we'll have a late lunch and take it easy for the rest of the day.'

She nodded, took one last deep breath, and all was under control.

'I shan't go outside. I'm pretty sure I scared off our friends the other night—I have no feeling of danger any more. And after tomorrow——' he shrugged. 'We'll have expert company.'

'Expert? No more so than you.'

He hung his head in mock modesty. 'Too kind,' he murmured.

'I mean it,' she said softly. 'I never felt afraid of any outside dangers—only for you, when you were out there—when it was not knowing——' she stopped and bit her lip.

'I know.' It was as if he did. 'You're like me, you prefer action. That's why I had to go out, you see.'

'Yes. It didn't make it any easier at the time, but I'd have done the same.'

'I believe you would.' It was said thoughtfully, after a brief pause, as if he had carefully considered it and found it to be true. 'In some ways, Joanna, we're alike.'

'I don't think so,' she said flatly. 'Our lives couldn't be more——' she hesitated, 'different.'

'I'm not talking about the lives we lead, I'm talking about inside us. What makes us tick.'

'And what makes you tick, then?'

He shrugged. 'Difficult to put into words, I suppose. I see through the sham, the false. I prefer to be doing rather than talking. I have my own set of rules—a code, if you prefer, and I try to live by it—no, this is ridiculous. I can't sum it up like that.'

'You weren't doing so badly,' she commented. 'But I'm not quite like that. I'm well aware of your real opinion of me, Roarke. You've made it clear—on occasions.' She lifted her head proudly. 'But you don't know the real me. I don't suppose you ever will.' She smiled, almost sadly. 'I've changed in these last few days. You might not believe that, and the results might not show, but I have. I've been made aware of the shallow emptiness of a lot of things. I don't know whether I've you to thank, or these surroundings, or perhaps a mixture of both. But I have realised, at last, why my father arranged this reunion.'

'Yes, I think you have. It was to——' a slight pause—
'save you. He cares, he has always cared about you,
followed your life closely, although you were never
aware of it, and he felt he had to do something before it
was too late. The way he chose was drastic, highly
dramatic, but it got you here, and that's what he wanted
above all else.'

'But why just me? What about my sister Laura?
You've never mentioned her.'

He shrugged. 'That's for him to tell you, Joanna.'

'I don't understand. Laura is my sister, she leads
the life I lead—or led——' she gave a wry grin at that.

'It's not quite the same thing.'

As she spoke next, she looked directly at him. 'You
know something, don't you?' His expression told her
the answer. 'Tell me,' she said. 'Tell me, because I can't
bear it.'

'He's your father, he's not hers.'

She knew. She had known all along in a part of her,
but the instinctive knowledge had been so deeply buried
inside her that it had never even surfaced. It was as if,
suddenly, all the pieces in a jigsaw fell into place when
the last one was touched. Laura was so like their mother,
much closer to her than Joanna had ever been, and what
Laura wanted Laura got, and had done so throughout
life, and would continue to do so. It explained so much,
so very much that Joanna hadn't even begun to understand all her life. She made a small hurt sound in her
throat, of anguish, and closed her eyes. 'Oh, dear God,'
she murmured. 'But I think I always knew.'

'Your mother had a lover when she was in her early
twenties—perhaps the only person she had ever really
loved, but he was a servant of your grandfather's, an
under-gardener. People of your mother's social standing
didn't do things like that—or if they did, they obeyed

the eleventh commandment: thou shalt not be found out. But she was—when she became pregnant. The man was bought off, presumably handsomely, for he vanished immediately—and your father, who was in love with her, and whose social status was impeccable, suddenly found himself accepted, and quietly married very soon after. The "premature" birth of your sister must have told him he'd been duped, but he was honourable; he said nothing, he made a good husband.

'Then, a year later, you were born. He had a daughter at last. You were and are in his image and he loved you dearly. They'd moved to England by this time, where his business interests lay, and then the ex-lover, the gardener, reappeared on the scene, and your mother took up where she'd left off before her hasty marriage. Your father gave her an ultimatum—and she chose her lover.'

'Oh, no!' Joanna felt profoundly sad.

'Your father knew that if he divorced her there would be a scandal that would be bound to affect your life—and it was you he cared for above all. Your mother was a good mother then—she had two pretty daughters, she had the money to see that you both had the best of everything. He simply took himself out of her life, and vanished. She told everyone, including presumably you and Laura, that he'd died at sea—he loved boats—and went her merry way.

'He quietly divorced her several years ago in Mexico and married my cousin Olivia. But he felt a great sadness at having abandoned you. He'd had no choice really. He could have fought a custody battle—but it would most likely gone against him and you would have been yet another grim statistic in the "tug of love" case that happens too often. He did what he thought best, but he looked after you from a distance as it were, and he saw how your life was changing in the past two or three years, and it concerned him deeply. So at last he decided to do something about it.'

He shrugged. 'And now you know the real reason why you're here.'

There was a long silence after he finished speaking. 'Thank you for telling me,' Joanna said quietly. 'It explains so very much.' There were tears in her eyes, but she wasn't going to cry, not again, like before. It was instead as though some part of her that had been missing all her life had been restored to her,

Roarke stood up. 'I'll make coffee,' he said quietly. 'Stay here, rest. You've had a few more shocks. It will take time——'

'Yes, I'll do that,' she answered. 'Thank you.' He went out and she was alone. He had used the word shocks. But they had not been exactly that. It had been almost a sensation of relief that had come over her when she had heard his story.

She wanted very much to meet her father. One day, that was all she had to wait. One more day.

# CHAPTER EIGHT

DURING the night a storm began, in the loneliest hours before dawn. Joanna awoke thinking that she was in the middle of a gigantic battlefield. Brilliant white light flashed through the window, jagged and frightening, to be followed almost immediately by the most devastating crashes of thunder. She wasn't scared, but she was sensible enough to know the dangers of tropical storms, so she got out of bed to go down and check that all the windows were safely shuttered. It took her fifteen minutes in the darkness, lit only with the shattering and fearsome crashes of light and sound, to make sure that all was as secure as it could be.

She had crept up the stairs again and paused at the top, wincing as yet another thunderflash rocked the house, when she saw a dark figure ahead of her starkly outlined in dazzling light, and caught her breath. He moved, and it was—of course—Roarke. 'Oh!' she gasped. 'I wasn't expecting to see you!'

'You've been down in this?' he asked.

'Yes.' She walked towards him. 'I went to check the shutters——'

'And I was just on my way to check the birds,' he answered. He was clad only in dark pyjama trousers. 'There's not a lot anyone can do, but I thought I'd give them some seed.'

'Yes. Look, while you do that, I'll make us a cup of coffee, shall I? I'm wide awake, I don't know about you.'

'Right. Find me a couple of aspirins while you're about it, will you? This kind of storm always gives me a headache.'

'I'll join you in those. Me too. You go up, I'll go down. See you in ten minutes.' Joanna ran back down again, found sufficient water was still in the kettle, and put it on. Instant coffee, powdered milk, and a bottle of aspirins seemed to be the ideal late night snack for the sophisticated jet-setter, and she laughed as she thought about it. She was feeling happier than she had done for longer than she could remember, but the reasons why were far too mixed up even to begin to wonder about then, at the lowest ebb of physical and mental energy; the hours before dawn, the hours of deepest sleep— rudely disturbed by the wild elements outside.

Joanna shivered slightly. It had gone very cold, and when the coffee was made, she carried it upstairs to- gether with the bottle of aspirin. Roarke was in his room, sitting on the bed. 'They were huddled together, away from the window,' he told her. 'Big ones and small ones, poor devils. I think they were glad to see me.'

She shook her head. 'It'll pass soon. They'll be all right, poor things.' She handed him his coffee. 'I was just thinking what riotous living we do. Coffee and two aspirins at some unearthly hour of the night! I'm not sure if I can keep this pace up!'

He laughed, then, as she shivered again, added: 'Are you cold?'

'Freezing. Aren't you?'

He shrugged. 'Ouch!' This as a stunning simultaneous flash and crash rocked the room. 'No, not particularly.' He touched her arm lightly. 'Mmm, so you are. Are you sure you feel all right?'

She wasn't too sure, actually. Odd, inexplicable things were happening to her. Shameful memories that she had managed to push away from her were not far away enough. It was due to a combination of factors, she knew; her recent fever, the knowledge about her father—

the lateness of the hour, and uppermost, the very primitive desire to be held safe and secure by the man she would always love with all her heart, whatever happened. 'I don't know,' she confessed, and she felt weak and vulnerable, and tried to fight it. She had been too weak recently, and part of her despised herself for giving in to the warmth of being looked after. She also felt very confused.

She swallowed two aspirins with coffee, and shivered again. 'Damn,' she muttered. 'This is stupid.'

The room was quite in darkness save for a light on the landing that she had put on to climb the stairs, and it cast a slanted beam through the open doorway.

'I can't offer you an electric blanket—nor even, alas, that great British comforter, a hot water bottle. For some absurd reason they're not considered necessary in jungles.'

'Good heavens!' she exclaimed. 'Do you mean you don't carry them on all your expeditions?'

'Not a one,' he replied solemnly.

'Oh. Remind me not to book one of your trips, then!' But even as she said it, it stopped being a joke. There was no danger that she would, ever . . .

A wave of coldness swept through her and it combined with a much nearer, much more frightening crash of thunder, and her hand jerked up, and coffee spilt all over her lap.

She yelled something and Roarke moved faster than any lightning, tore the nightgown off, and wrapped his sheet around her. His action was so swift that only a small amount had actually penetrated through to her skin. He ran into the bathroom and came back with a flannel, and Joanna pressed it on to her thigh, and gasped.

'Lie down,' he ordered, and she obeyed. 'Where did it go?'

'Just here—where the flannel is. That was quick, Roarke, thank you.'

'Stay still. I'll be back in seconds.' He was gone. The skin tingled and throbbed, but the coffee hadn't been boiling, and the cold water had effectively cooled her, and she was still so stunned by the speed with which everything had happened that she lay back, bemused.

He came in carrying a tube of cream and gave it to her. She had covered herself modestly with the sheet in his absence, and he turned away as she applied the cream gently to a large scalded patch on her inner thigh. 'Ah! Ouch!' she muttered. 'Oh! That's much better.'

He turned back to her and sat down beside where she lay in his bed. 'You're just a walking disaster area,' he said. 'What are we going to do with you?'

His words were light and joking, as had his other comments been, about hot water bottles, and the atmosphere should have been as normal as it was possible to be, under the circumstances, but it wasn't—and they both knew it. It was not only outside that the air was filled with electric, vibrant currents. They were also there in the room as she lay, and he sat, on the bed. The very air buzzed with it and Joanna could scarcely breathe. Desire swirled round them, an invisible mist that held memories . . .

She tried to speak, to answer, but she couldn't, and a tremor of such intensity caught her that she shook with it. She must go, she knew that, and Roarke knew it too, but neither moved.

Then he spoke. His voice had gone slightly deeper, almost husky. 'Let me check that you're all right.' He lifted the sheet fractionally, so far, no farther, but his hand was shaking too.

'It's—it's—fine,' she croaked. Her heartbeats rocked her body.

'Yes, it is. Good.'

She swallowed hard, and cleared her throat. 'Er—I'd better go.'

'Yes, yes of course.' He cleared his throat as well. His hand was still on her thigh, and he didn't seem aware of the fact. 'Yes, you must go.'

'Will you—help me up?' she managed to say.

'Of course.' He lifted her, and the sheet fell away as he did so, and she sat and faced him, and they both reached for it at the same time, but Roarke got it first and lifted it to cover her breasts and accidentally touched her—he stopped, and then, as if he couldn't help it, smoothed his warm hand very gently over her skin, then cupped the sweet naked roundness in his hand. He moved towards her, put his other hand behind her bare back, and held her closely as he caressed her breasts with trembling fingers.

'Roarke, I——' she gasped. 'I—don't think—you should be doing this.' But it was a token protest, no more than that. Her body flamed with the urgent desire for him and she knew that his need for her was as fiery and urgent.

His only response was to kiss her, to put his demanding mouth over hers and silence her protests, and then to push her gently down so that he lay with her.

'Be careful—my scald——' she whispered, and he said huskily:

'Oh, my darling, I will be very careful, very, very careful——' and he touched her with the tender, gentle hands she had known so well, once—twice, recently, and she pulled his head down to her mouth and kissed him to tell him, to let him know that her need was as great as his. Her soft lips yielded to his, and the love she knew for him welled up inside her, filling her body with a warmth she had never known before.

The sensuous caresses of skilful fingers was a delight to her and all thoughts of right and wrong had long since ceased to matter as their naked bodies melted together and they pleasured each other in new, beautiful ways and yielded to the growing, urgent excitement that filled them both.

There was no one else in the whole world. Their world was each other. The crashing crescendoes of the thunder and the brilliant shafts of lightning accompanied their quickening movements and were welcomed almost as friends.

And at last they slept, now no longer cold. The storm had gone, and all was quiet save for their breathing, and the matching heartbeats.

It was light when they awoke. Sun streamed through the windows as they both opened their eyes. Roarke looked at her and ran his hands down her pliant body, and said: 'I shan't be fit for anything today.'

'No regrets?' she whispered.

'None. It's too late for that anyway. I want you more than I've ever wanted any woman in my life—but you must know that.'

She smiled faintly. 'I did rather get the message. I needed you, Roarke, I'm not ashamed to admit it. I wanted you very much to make love to me. If that makes me sound like a wanton hussy, then that's what I am.'

'Hussy?' He savoured the word slowly. 'I like that. Hussy Joanna. As a title it suits you.' He sobered. 'Oh, God, we shouldn't have. Remember you accused me when I first "abducted" you of wanting to rape you and how annoyed I was?' She nodded. 'I really *was* annoyed. It seems that you were right after all. What do I do to apologise?'

'I'll think of something,' she teased, and stroked his chest. 'Mmm, yes, I could think of something right now.'

'Don't do that,' he groaned.

'Do what? This,' she giggled, 'or *this*?'

He grabbed her hand. 'For God's sake, Joanna, don't! I can't——'

'Can't? I thought that wasn't a word in your vocabulary?'

'I might have to make an exception in this case. I am but a weak man, unhand me at once——' She put her lips to his and ran her tongue along them.

'Ssh,' she scolded. 'Be quiet!'

Roarke lifted his hand, leaving a trail of fire across her body. 'You'll be sorry,' he said huskily. 'You should never start anything you can't finish——' and he took her to him again and then proceeded to demonstrate very effectively that 'can't' was certainly a word *not* in his vocabulary.

Later, they showered and dressed, then waited for her father and stepmother to arrive. Joanna was a new woman. She glowed. She knew she would never be the same again. Roarke, since entering her life, had changed it in more ways then she could ever begin to count. She moved in a dream of love and warmth that owed nothing to the day, but was within her.

Roarke, too, was different. Gone was the bitter tension of their first hours. She couldn't understand that she had found him aggressive and potentially violent. It seemed impossible.

He had made a final radio check with her father, and they had lunch together knowing that it would be their last meal alone. By the evening John and Olivia would have arrived. The devastating storm of the night had left its toll in shattered trees, and branches and leaves littered the space surrounding the house. Roarke had brought the helicopter down the previous day from its roof perch—fortunately, as he told Joanna, for it could have provided a focal point for the jagged-edged lightning. He could not explain why he had done so, except that he must have subconsciously sensed a brewing storm. That too was covered, almost camouflaged, with the debris of the storm.

After lunch he went out, stripped to the waist, to clear as much as he could, particularly to leave a patch for her father's helicopter to land on. He would not allow Joanna to help, so she stood at the door, drinking in the sweet cool air that was also a legacy of the storm, and watched him work. She was constantly alert to any danger signs, but there were none. Roarke used a large leafy branch in the manner of a broom, sweeping aside shattered wood, cutting a wide swathe with his improvised brush, and the sweat ran down his chest and arms in rivulets, and he was streaked and black when he had finally finished. He flung his makeshift broom into the trees and came towards her, face tired. 'That's it,' he announced, and wiped his face with his hand, streaking it even more with dirt.

'If you go and have a shower—and you need one,' she told him, 'I'll make you a delicious drink.'

'That sounds like an offer I can't refuse,' he said, grimacing as he looked down at himself.

'Don't look in a mirror,' she warned. 'Your face is even worse.'

'Thanks.' He scowled at her. 'I needed that comment.' He slapped her bottom as she passed him in the hall. 'Go and make that drink, hussy, and do something useful for a change.'

'Huh!' She stalked off laughing to the kitchen.

All was ready. She began to feel restless, even faintly apprehensive, heart beating faster in anticipation of what was to come. Then from somewhere far away, and high in the sky, came the first slight sounds of an approaching helicopter. Roarke heard it first, then Joanna, and they both went to the door and stood on the steps. He put his arm around her.

'Scared?' he teased.

'Yes, a little.'

'You needn't be. He loves you, Joanna, remember that. He always has.'

'Yes.' She said it very quietly, and his arm tightened fractionally around her. Then they saw it, high, high, above the towering trees and coming nearer and larger with every moment. They neither of them spoke, but she felt almost dazed with the sensations that filled her. At last, the man who was her father, who had arranged her abduction at the hands of Roarke, was arriving. He had been delayed by illness, and in a strange way that had altered her life too, for Roarke had been instrumental in making her see so much, that she had already changed inwardly beyond recognition. All within the space of a few days she had had her eyes opened to the awareness of a richer life—that had no connection with material wealth. She would not have thought it possible to see the world so differently, but she did.

The giant bird hovered, quivering, above then began its descent, rotor blades whirling, then slowing imperceptibly until they clattered to a halt, and the door of the helicopter opened.

Roarke and Joanna went forward, he leading her, she trembling and unsure of herself, and a tall, very dark man jumped down and grinned at Roarke, then turned to help a woman down. She too was tall, as tall as Joanna, and dark and attractive, possibly in her early forties. She looked at Joanna and smiled as she came forward, and Joanna returned the smile, but her wide eyes went back irresistibly to the helicopter, for now a man was emerging. Slightly bent, he was assisted out by the strong arms of the dark man, and Joanna shook herself free of Roarke's gentle hold and went forward, compelled by something stronger than she knew, and looked into the clear blue eyes of the tall, grey-haired man who was her father, put her arms around him, oblivious to anyone else's presence, and said: 'Oh, Father, I can't tell you how wonderful——' Her voice broke.

John Cunningham held her gently, his eyes dimmed with his own tears, his voice shaky.

'Joanna, my dear child, at last!'

Crying, laughing, they walked back towards the house. She supposed that Roarke and the others were following, but it did not seem to impinge on her consciousness too much. She was vividly aware only of the man who walked slowly beside her, and she matched her steps to his, for he was newly out of hospital, and convalescent.

They entered the house, went into the drawing room where both sat down on the settee and looked properly for the first time at each other, and held hands, she like a small child, in wonder and trust, he with a hold gentle and caring, as if she might break in two.

'Oh, Joanna, my dearest girl, this is really you at last, after all these years,' he said. 'Do you forgive me for doing what I did to get you here?'

She shook her head. 'There's nothing to forgive. I know why you did it. I know everything—and you were so right. How right I'll try and tell you, but it might take days.' She laughed. 'I'm so happy!'

'You look it. You look radiant, Joanna, truly radiant. You're a very beautiful young woman—and I'm sure you've been told that before, but you must indulge an old man who's only seen you from a distance—and in photographs.'

She looked at him. 'From a distance? Do you mean——'

He smiled wryly. 'I watched you through binoculars last year, from the balcony of a hotel in Cannes. You were on the deck of a yacht. I watched for quite a while, but of course you were never aware of it. I think it was then that I formulated my little plot for your kidnap——' he shook his head. 'But we'll talk much more later. You must meet Olivia, and Eddie and Donald, who are my "team" as you might say.' He patted her hand. 'I think I hear them in the kitchen. They're all being extremely tactful, allowing new father and daughter to get acquainted, but, as you say, we have time to talk, all the time we need, and we will, later on.'

'Are you well, Father? I don't want you to be tired on my account.'

'I'm tough, my love, I'm a tough old man, and nothing, but *nothing*, was going to stop me getting here today. Yes, I need rest, but that will pass.'

'And you're not old either,' she said indignantly. 'Please don't say that!'

'I don't feel it,' he admitted. 'Well—perhaps at the moment, after a long, two-stage journey from Rio, but that too will pass. You make me feel young again. We have so much to catch up on, so many lost years, but I promise you, my dear, we will not be separated again.'

'And my life is changed,' she said quietly. 'You'll see. I know the emptiness——' she paused. He squeezed her hand.

'Not now,' he said, equally soft-voiced. 'It's strange, isn't it, how things can change? A year ago I wouldn't have dreamed this reunion possible—and now we're here, together after more than twenty years, and it's as if we've known each other all your life. I am a truly contented man. Come,' he stood up, 'let me introduce you to your stepmother.'

They went slowly into the kitchen. Olivia sat at the table drinking coffee, while the two men were stocking the refrigerator with food. Roarke was brewing more coffee, and all four were laughing and talking like the old friends they clearly were.

Olivia stood and came towards the door as they entered, touching her husband's cheek and then embracing Joanna. 'Hello, love,' she said. It was a warm, caring gesture, and her voice too radiated her inner qualities of kindness. Joanna liked her instantly.

'Hello,' she responded. 'May I call you Olivia?'

The older woman laughed. 'Of course. What else? If you dare to call me stepmother, I'll not speak to you again!' She turned. 'Meet Eddie and Donald, our friends and companions on many journeys.'

Joanna went across to them. Eddie, clearly the pilot, was a stocky man of perhaps fifty, grey-haired and blue-eyed with a ruddy complexion. He grinned at her as he took her hand. 'Pleased to meet you, Joanna,' he said. He had a very down-to-earth, no-nonsense Yorkshire accent.

Donald, younger, taller, darker, was the man who had helped both Olivia and her father from the helicopter. Whipcord-thin, he had dark hair and intense brown eyes. His handshake reflected his great strength. 'Hi,' he said. 'In case they don't tell you, I'm the photographer and general brains behind the system around here,' a remark which was greeted with hoots of derisive laughter. His accent was pure Texan, and his eyes held more than a spark of interest as he looked at Joanna. She was also aware that Roarke was watching the introduction, casually—or apparently so—with the merest flicker of amusement added.

'We're going to eat soon,' Olivia announced. 'If you gentlemen would care to leave us, Joanna and I will prepare a meal.'

As the others went out, she turned and winked at Joanna. 'You don't have to help,' she said, 'but I think they'd like to have a natter together now they're all met up again——'

'I'd love to help,' Joanna answered. 'I'm not an expert

cook, but I'll do exactly as I'm told.'

'Let's finish our coffee first. There's no hurry. We brought some fine old brandy with us. They'll be enjoying that, and cigars. You'll see—when we go in the air will be blue with smoke.'

Olivia sat down and regarded Joanna very steadily. 'I know that what we did was quite outrageous,' she said. 'And I was expecting to meet a perfect little bitch today, as spoilt as they come. I'm speaking frankly because I always do—and you have every right to be equally blunt with me—but I'll tell you now, you've let me down!' She paused momentarily, then gave an impish grin. 'I fully expected not to like you—but it's impossible. I think you're super, and I'm going to love being your stepmama, so there!'

Joanna sat down more slowly. The words had a strange effect; a sadness mingling with happiness. Days ago, Olivia would not have been disappointed. She would have met the spoilt little bitch that she had expected to meet. Then Joanna smiled. 'I've changed since coming here. Roarke is a wise man, Olivia. He's made me see so much in a few days.'

'Has he? Yes, I can believe that.' Olivia's eyes grew soft. 'He's a hard, uncompromising man, my cousin, but he's also possibly the sanest man I've ever met. Our mothers are sisters, and very close, and so are we. You couldn't have had a better "kidnapper", although I say it myself!'

Joanna wondered about Roarke. She wanted so much to hear everything about him, but she didn't want to give herself away. The feelings she had for Roarke were intense and very private. She had no idea if any of them were returned. He was a powerful, virile and exciting lover, but she wasn't naïve enough to assume that he had fallen head over heels because he had made love to her. They had wanted each other—the inevitable had happened. Yet Joanna's own love for him was great enough for her to want his happiness above all. She wondered if she would ever see him again after he left. She wanted to, more than anything, but she had learned enough over the last few precious days to know that he was a free spirit, a wanderer in strange unknown places.

He had been caring and kind during her brief weakness of the fever. She could easily have misinterpreted it as affection returned, but that was something else she had learned. He was so truly different from any man she had ever known in her life before and his reactions were not the same as other, lesser mortals. She wanted him with all her heart, but he would have to be the one to let her know his feelings; hers would be kept well hidden, for safety—and for her own self-respect.

She answered Olivia's joking comment with one equally humorous, and they began to prepare a feast for the four men. Conversation flowed easily as they worked, the atmosphere harmonious between the two women. This was another new experience for Joanna. The highly competitive world she had so recently left meant never being able to relax. There was a brittle edge to all verbal exchanges, wherever, at parties, social gatherings, anywhere she was. That was the way of life as she knew it. It explained the cool, wary look on the faces of so many jet-setters, a bland hardness of expression, laughter carefully gauged so that it was neither too loud, nor could cause too many wrinkles in beautiful skin. Olivia knew no such restrictions. Her laughter was infectious, pealing out, and the laughter lines around her eyes were more beautiful than unlined smoothness.

Joanna was relaxed as she had never been able to be with another woman—not even her own mother. She didn't pause to see why this should be so, she just knew it to be true.

They all ate together in the dining room and the

men—totally and pleasantly relaxed after their brandies and cigars—made an interesting quartet of male admirers for both women. It was a very enjoyable meal.

Joanna assumed that Roarke had put the three men completely up to date with the situation regarding the disappearing servants, and the headhunters, but no mention of it was made during or after dinner when they all returned to the drawing room for coffee and liqueurs. Outside, the darkness, long since fallen, was a cloak wrapped round the large house, and no longer hostile. She was tired, struggling to keep awake, but her father saw, and said quietly to her across the ebb and flow of the conversation, 'Joanna, you must go to bed, you know. Roarke told me you'd not been well.'

'What about you?' she protested weakly.

'I shall be retiring very soon, my dear. Doctor's orders, alas, but *you*, I'm giving you *father's* orders. To bed!'

She laughed. 'How can I refuse that?' She stood up and kissed him. 'I'll go now. If you'll all excuse me?'

She sallied forth with the various goodnights ringing in her ears, and went to her bedroom. It was just after ten, but five minutes after putting her head on the pillow she was soundly asleep.

When she awoke and went down the following morning, her father and Olivia were the only ones in the house. Eddie, Donald and Roarke had gone out to check on everything, and had already been gone more than an hour, her father told her. He was in the drawing room, and Olivia told them she had several jobs to do, and left them. Joanna had no doubt that this was merely a tactful move on her stepmother's part to enable them to talk, and as soon as she had gone Joanna's father began to tell her of all that had happened over the years, confirming in one way what Roarke had already said, but adding more that only he could know. He spoke in a gentle, caring way, each word considered, and she listened, her heart saddened yet filled with love for him. He was her father. To state that simply to herself, every so often, was a warm and wonderful thing. Her father. Found after a lifetime, and here with her, and loving her as she loved him. It was good, it was very good.

They were not aware of time passing, of Olivia fetching cool drinks in, or of the three men returning. The morning passed in a blur of sound and colour and images, both talking at their times, both listening when it was needed. And so much was said, so much richness and love that it enfolded them both, and Joanna felt as if that part of her which had always been missing had been restored to her.

The evening of the day passed without the intensity of the morning, for so much had been said that it was enough for one day. And it was late in that evening that Roarke told them that he would have to leave the following day. As he spoke he looked at Joanna, and she let not a flicker of any emotion show. She even managed to smile. Olivia exclaimed: 'Oh, Roarke! We never see you for long. I suppose you've a crowd of blue-rinsed Yankee matrons waiting for you in Sao Paulo or something?'

'Or something,' he agreed drily. 'Six Australians looking for a lost Inca city.' He paused. 'It's been discovered a dozen times in the last century—a fact they know—but they're sure *they'll* be the ones to find the Inca gold no one else could.' He shrugged. 'So, off on the merry-go-round again.'

Joanna's father chuckled. 'You make them new, each time,' he remarked. 'Very interesting and entertaining. Remember that trip I went on? I enjoyed myself immensely.'

'I laid on a few extras for you, John. It's not often I

get distinguished visitors, you know.'

'Ah, I see. A con man!'

'Something like that,' Roarke agreed, with a grin and a wink at Olivia. Joanna waited for the moment when she could go to bed without making it obvious that she would be escaping from an intolerable situation. She felt shattered. She had known that he had to leave, but to hear it so casually, in the company of everyone, was like a slap in the face. She was adept at hiding her feelings—she had had years of training, but the new Joanna, newly vulnerable, loving, ached with the pain of it.

Dear God, she thought. I wish I didn't know. Let him go, just go. It was as though another part of her was being torn away.

She went out to the kitchen, her offer to make a coffee being accepted by all. There she filled the kettle to make coffee, and she felt ill and shivery and she knew it was because she loved Roarke, and there was absolutely nothing she could do about it.

'Hi;' Olivia's voice came from the door. 'Can I help?'

'Of course—thanks.' She turned to the other woman, relieved at not having to be alone with her thoughts.

'Something wrong?' enquired Olivia softly, dark eyes filled with motherly concern.

Joanna shook her head, but couldn't for the moment answer. 'Oh dear,' said Olivia softly. 'It's Roarke, isn't it?'

Joanna bit her lip. Then, slowly, she nodded. 'Is it so obvious?' she whispered.

'No, love.' Olivia chuckled. 'Not one bit. But I've got sharp eyes. I saw your over-cool reaction when he said he was leaving. Look, my sweet, I love him dearly, and he's something special, but be thankful he's going——'

Joanna turned to her, wide-eyed with disbelief, and Olivia pulled a wry face. 'I'm sorry to have to say it, but I have now. You might as well know—he'll never love any woman. He was let down badly, once, years ago, and he vowed never to fall in love again, and he hasn't. He's had affairs, I'm sure, but oh, my dear, he'll never settle down. I'm only telling you this because you're my husband's daughter, and I love John more than life itself—and I want you to be happy too, because that will make him happy—I also love Roarke, as I said, but I see his faults, and his major one is—women,' She smiled. 'But it's not too late, thank heavens.'

Oh, isn't it? thought Joanna. Olivia wasn't as wise as she thought. She had said what she had from a warm concern, and undoubtedly thought that Joanna was mildly infatuated, no more. How wrong she was she would never know. Joanna took a deep breath.

'Thanks for the warning,' she answered lightly. 'As you say, it's not too late. I find him attractive—what woman wouldn't? But——' she shrugged, 'he leaves tomorrow. I'll say goodbye happily.'

'That's my girl!' Olivia smiled. 'I don't know how long you can stay here, but you're welcome for as long as you like—sorry about the clothes, love, I had to get something fast when we knew the plan was on. If you want Eddie to fly you to your friends for your luggage, you just tell me.'

'I'll manage,' Joanna assured her, 'and I'd like to stay a week or more, at least.' She paused. 'By the time I leave I'll have altered my social calendar quite a lot.'

Olivia watched her, calm and assured. She knew, that was why, but she waited for Joanna to tell her. Joanna went on more quietly: 'I've seen so many things differently since I came here—and my father's arrival just set the seal on the change. I've finished with my jet-set existence—oh, Olivia, you can't imagine how shallow it all is, and how long it's taken me to see it.' She sat down at the table. 'I'm going to get a job of some sort. Not for the money; possibly something voluntary. I don't know what yet, but I've given it a great deal of thought—I'll find something.'

'There's a lot to be done everywhere,' agreed Olivia. 'Your father has done so much for so many people, and animals—he'd kill me if he heard me telling you, but I don't care. Anything he does is wonderful. He supports a children's home near Rio—that's where we'd been when he was taken ill—there's also the work he does for animals, endangered species——' Joanna nodded, remembering Roarke's words on that, 'and he cares so deeply about so many things. He could be a millionaire many times over, but he doesn't want to be. He's happier giving it away to those who never stand a chance in life.'

Joanna's eyes filled with tears, and Olivia put her arms around her shoulders. 'Don't cry, love,' she said mildly. 'There's nothing to cry about. He is as he is because he's a wonderful man. And Roarke, bless his heart, helps him a lot.'

'Roarke?' He had never said anything about that.

Olivia smiled wryly. 'Hmm, he wouldn't tell, would he? But he does, I promise you. He cares too, in his own different way, but no one knows, except your father and me.'

'He's writing a book about his expeditions,' said Joanna. 'I've been helping him with the typing. It was something to keep me occupied when things were dangerous—he's led a fascinating life.'

'That's true. He's a loner in a way, is Roarke. A man who walks happily through life independent of others' approval or disapproval. He doesn't need it, you see. And that's how he will always be.'

Joanna knew that already with her own deep sure love for him; she knew how he was. It didn't alter her feelings in any way except perhaps to clarify them. She owed him a great debt, and always would, but in a way, she would repay it, even if he never knew. Olivia's words on his attitude to women had been a surprise and a shock—but only for moments. She knew the deep truth of them, now that they had been absorbed. They fitted into the image she had of him, stored in her heart.

What a strange world it is, she thought. And that was still in her mind, when, later on, she escaped to bed, very tired with all the events of the day.

She lay in bed trying vainly to sleep when the tap came at the door. Even before she answered it, she knew who it would be.

# CHAPTER NINE

'COME in,' Joanna answered, and Roarke entered, closing the door behind him. He walked soft-footed to the bed. She, watching him, wondered who the woman had been who had hurt him so badly.

'I've come to say goodbye,' he told her. 'I've decided to leave at first light.'

'Of course,' she said calmly, in control. 'Sit on the bed.' She had switched on the light. Whatever had been between them—and it had been tempestuous—was over. Both knew it, both accepted it. Something had changed, and nothing would ever be the same again, but the brief episode that had changed her life was over. She was enriched by it, she loved him dearly, and she ached to have him hold her, but outwardly she faced him with great serenity, and even managed to smile at him. 'Thank you for bringing me here. I didn't feel like thanking you at the beginning—as you know—but now I've met my father, I do with all my heart.' He bowed his head slightly as if in acknowledgment. 'And please— get your book typed. It's good.'

His mouth twitched. 'I'll accept your judgment on that. I will, I promise—when I have time to get it done.' He paused, and looked at her, and she looked back at him, and the tension that she could feel in the room, surrounding them, was obviously all in her own imagination, so she fought to suppress it, to make the atmosphere as light as it must be.

'I'll be staying for another week or so,' she said quietly—and quickly, because any silence might be more than she could bear. 'Then I'll be off. But I'll see my father as often as I can in the future——'

'And where will you go when you leave here?' he asked, much as he might have enquired somebody's opinion of the weather.

'I don't know. I'm altering my plans a lot——' she paused, then plunged on: 'Since meeting my father.' And you, she added, but only to herself.

'I see.' Roarke stood up. It seemed as if the conversation was over. 'I wish you luck, Joanna.'

'And you, Roarke.' The air shimmered with the tension that filled it, and he stood facing her, she sitting up in bed, her soft blonde hair framing her face—her eyes hiding her love for him, her skin golden and glowing. He, dark, tall, powerful, a deep complex man who might have affairs but would never love any woman—never love her in return. A gulf as wide as an ocean lay between them and would never be breached. She held out her hand. 'Goodbye.'

He came forward to take it, to grip hard and cool. 'Goodbye, Joanna.' He walked away from her, reached the door and opened it. For an instant he paused as if he might be about to say something—then he went out, closing the door softly but with a kind of finality, after him.

Joanna lay back and let the tears flow freely.

The next few days passed at leisurely pace, and there was a kind of magic to them even despite the void left after Roarke's departure. Joanna and her father were getting to know each other properly after the wasted years, and each day brought new wonders of recognition. Olivia was tact itself, never intrusive, but caring and clearly delighting in Joanna's company. Both Eddie and Donald were busy building a run outside the house. John intended to study some small jungle monkeys, and an enclosed pen would enable him to do so more easily.

He was recovering quickly from his operation, alert and alive and more vital every day.

The reappearance of the two servants surprised no one except Joanna, and Olivia said with a grin: 'That means all danger's over. They have some kind of jungle alarm that we're too stupid to hear. One day we might, and then we'll learn a lot more.'

The routine was resumed as ever it had been, the house smoothly running, everyone with their share of work to do, and doing it. Both Donald and Eddie were pleasant company. Donald was clearly attracted to Joanna, but never behaved in a way that might have made her uncomfortable. She liked him, and one afternoon they walked through trees to reach a tributary of the Amazon which lay only a short way from the house.

It was steamy and humid near the water, with sullen swirls and currents lending menace to the dark river. Birds darted over the surface, skimming, touching, catching the flies that swarmed near its banks, and there were hidden dangers there, that was obvious.

Donald looked down at her. 'Care for a swim?' he teased.

'No, thanks!' she shuddered. 'What a thought!'

He laughed. 'See that log over there?' He pointed, taking her arm casually to guide her. She looked.

'Yes.'

'Keep your eyes on it.' He bent, picked up a pebble and flicked it expertly over the water to land on the log—which promptly reared up, large tail thrashing— and turned out to be an alligator.

'Oh, my God!' she exclaimed. An impressive sight, the alligator glared balefully at them and launched itself away with a final contemptuous sweep of its tail.

'You were taking a chance,' she remarked dryly. 'They come ashore, don't they?'

'Occasionally. But they're not so stupid—or so vicious—as people try to make out. They much prefer to be left alone to bask in the sun—and why not?' He grinned. 'Anyway, I'm a whizz at climbing trees. How about you?'

'With the right incentive, yes,' she agreed.

'Let's go back,' he suggested. 'Careful!' this as a hidden branch nearly tripped Joanna up. He held her arm, a friendly gesture, no more, but lingered after, and his touch was warm and gentle. She didn't want him to hold her. He was an attractive man, no doubt about that, and she would have enjoyed a flirtation with him under any other circumstances, and it might be better if she could. One sure way of getting a man out of the system was to replace him with another, as she had found out frequently. But she had never loved a man before, so intensely and so deeply, and while it was a pain and an anguish it was also a revelation to her of the depth of feeling of which she was capable. She moved his hand gently away with a smile of pure friendliness, because in a moment he intended to kiss her, and she didn't want that either.

'Mmm,' he said thoughtfully. 'Old-fashioned girl?'

'That's me.' She looked up at him. 'Sorry, Don.'

'Roarke?' he asked very softly.

She stiffened. 'What do you mean?'

'No offence, Joanna. Just a guess.'

'Well, I'd rather you didn't guess anything about me.'

'Sorry. Forget I spoke.'

'Done.' She had recovered fast. It seemed to be obvious to everyone—and that was rather disturbing, but Donald was so pleasant that she couldn't feel angry with him. Another change in her. She had always possessed—and not been afraid to use—a caustic tongue when the occasion demanded. It no longer seemed important to score off anyone as she once would have done. She took his arm. 'There. Friends again?'

He laughed. 'Damn his eyes! Your father should have asked me to abduct you.' He grinned down at her. 'You're eminently fanciable, and I'm a normal male. If I didn't think I'd get my face slapped, I'd chance a kiss. Even worse—I might find myself flying. Roarke told me how you nearly got him coming out of the 'copter.'

'Did he?' What else might he have told? 'Did he also say that he counter-moved equally fast?'

'I've seen him in action. He didn't need to. But he admired your guts. He was impressed.'

'I wasn't aware I'd been the subject of your conversations,' she said.

Donald stopped walking. It was clear that something in her voice had reached him, for he said softly: 'That was all. Just to clarify things.'

'Really?'

'That's it—really.' Their eyes met and in his was nothing save the desire to explain to her.

Joanna softened. 'I'm sorry.' She shook her head. 'I'm stupid.'

'You're probably tired. You've had your life turned upside down, finding your father—coming here against your will. You're certainly not stupid, Joanna. I'll miss you when you go. You're like a breath of fresh English air to this jaded Texan.'

'Why, thank you, sah,' she drawled in an accurate imitation of his Texas tones, and he laughed delightedly.

'Shucks, ma'am, that wus really good.'

She bobbed a curtsey. 'Where are you going when you leave?' he asked.

'I've been thinking about it. I want to do something completely different. My stepmother was telling me of a place in Rio, a children's home—I'm not sure if I'd have the stamina to work there, but I'd like to try.'

He shook his head. 'Nope. Don't even think about it—yet.'

'What on earth do you mean?'

He stared at her thoughtfully. They were within sight of the house, in the clearing, and both stopped walking as by mutual consent, as if there were things to be said that would be better said there. 'I don't know how to put this,' Donald said, 'without appearing to be offensive—but I'll try. You're used to one kind of world. You've never encountered grinding poverty, have you? Except perhaps from the safety of a car or train, being whisked through some shanty town. But I'll bet you've never *been* there. I have, Joanna. I spent weeks helping to build new dormitories at La Placa, and I'm tough, and I don't give a damn because I've seen it all in my thirty-one years of life, and lived some, but I hadn't seen anything like that, and I cried, Joanna, one night there when they brought in a little scrap of humanity, a boy, no more than three or four, who was starvin' and so filthy that you couldn't tell whether he was black or white, and his belly was swollen with malnutrition. I went out of that room and I wept some—and I ain't never done that before.' He took a deep breath. 'Olivia didn't weep. She set to with the nuns, feeding him glucose and warm milk, and washing him, and she stayed with him for forty-eight hours solid, never left his side, and she nursed him back to life. That took the kind of guts a lot of us ain't got.'

Joanna, rooted to the spot, was so shaken by his story that for a moment she literally could not speak. The picture he painted was painful, vivid and raw, and his assessment of her was correct. Nothing like that had ever impinged on her existence before. She looked towards the house and Olivia was walking down the steps towards them, clad in casual trousers and yellow blouse, her dark hair neatly tied with a scrap of pale yellow ribbon. She waved at them. Joanna looked at Donald.

'Thank you,' she said. 'I'm going to have a word with Olivia. All you've said has moved me. I don't suppose I can ever hope to do what Olivia's done. All I know is— I'd like to try. I might be doing something useful with my life for once, who knows?'

He touched her arm. 'Then go to it, gal! It's up to you.'

She smiled faintly at him as Olivia reached them. 'So it is.' She took her stepmother's arm. 'I know where I'm going when I leave here. May we talk? I think we need to.'

'Of course.' They walked on together to the house. Donald loped after them, a bemused and bewildered man. They left him and went together into the kitchen, and there Joanna began to speak. She told Olivia what she wanted to do, and while at first Olivia listened with doubt and faint scepticism, after a while she did no longer.

The disappearance of Joanna Crozier from the gossip columns was not at first noticed. After all, it is far easier to spot who is in them than who is *not* mentioned, and only her immediate circle of friends were aware that she no longer appeared in the fashionable places. To them she had, quite simply, gone mad. Stories of her going to work in the jungle surfaced briefly and then were forgotten as newer people, new excitements, came to take her place. In three months it was as though she had never existed.

She knew this would be happening. She had no illusions about her jet-set circle. In June, when she should have been watching the tennis at Wimbledon, she was in her second month at the orphanage outside Rio de Janeiro, and she was too busy to think about anything save her immediate surroundings.

Donald had been accurate in his story. The dismay

she felt when she first arrived had been a shock wave. She could not understand how people could live in the conditions that lay beyond the orphanage walls.

Filthy shanty houses, made of cardboard and branches and strips of torn lino garnered from heaven knew where, were home to families of up to a dozen people. Streets ran with open sewage and debris, and children foraged for scraps alongside rats in the rutted tracks.

The Mother Superior, Mother Teresa, an Irishwoman with an ageless face, was a practical woman who wasted no time on sentimentality or moralising, but got on with her work. She regarded Joanna, as the daughter of their benefactor, with mixed feelings. Joanna, knowing this, knowing too that it was important to herself that she did not fail, told the elderly nun frankly about her life, and the reasons for her coming there, and finished with the words: 'I will do anything that you ask me to do. I want to prove that I mean it.'

The nun gave her a smile, a very wise smile. 'Then we'll see, my child. You will be tired, and saddened, and disillusioned—and you will also work harder than you have ever done in your life. I will not spare you, because to do so would be to insult you. The greatest compliment I can pay you is to treat you exactly as I do the other workers here.'

That was how it had begun, and had continued. It had taken her only a few days to settle in. The orphanage was a haven in the midst of turmoil. A large house and stables were the main buildings, but more were being built to accommodate the growing numbers of children. In several acres of land, the entire place was surrounded by a whitewashed wall that had become a landmark, an oasis. Joanna found herself more than once, and much to her surprise, lending a hand on the practical side of hammering nails into planks, studying plans as if she had been doing it all her life.

Local labour was recruited for the heavy work, the men glad to earn some money, but they needed constant supervision to keep them at their labours. Joanna lived for most of the time in jeans and shirts and sandals. Her hair had grown long, bleached by the sun, her skin was deeply tanned—and she would have been completely unrecognisable to any of her friends. She ate the simplest fare, with the children, and she had channelled several thousand pounds of her money into the orphanage so that further improvements could be made.

Her father, Olivia, Eddie and Donald turned up unexpectedly one week, and stayed to work. She was overjoyed to see them, and led them through the courtyard to the main house, followed by the usual cluster of small children, to whom she was 'Zho-arna'.

She was needed here; no one had ever needed her before. Roarke filled her dreams, but not her waking moments—for there was no time. She had always been healthy despite a life of lazy lotus-eating; now, with hard work and a spartan regime and diet, her body was fitter and healthier than ever. She had forgotten what make-up was for. Her only beauty accessories were soap and comb.

She had planned to stay there for three months, and then, as Olivia had advised, have a change. It seemed wise, and Joanna decided she would return to England for a rest and a rethink, after another visit to her father. It was arranged that she would fly to Manaos in September, where Eddie would pick her up and take her to her father's house.

It was a terrible day when she left the orphanage. She felt the wrench of leaving the children, and promised that she would return soon. She had, during her time there, arranged for every child to have a new outfit—simple shifts in unbleached cotton for the girls, equally simple shorts and shirts for the boys—and all were newly arrayed as they waved her off. The Mother Superior kissed her warmly on both cheeks. 'You have been a wonderful help to us, Joanna, in so many ways,' she said. 'We will all miss you.'

'I'll miss all of you too.' Joanna choked back the tears. 'But I'll be back, I promise.'

She flew out of Rio with drawings from all the children clutched in her hands, and slept all the way holding them. Eddie was waiting for her at Manaos, greeted her with a hug, and whisked her off to the helicopter.

She slept for two days at the house, interrupted only by necessary visits to the bathroom, and for cold drinks. It was the sleep of utter exhaustion, but when she surfaced at the beginning of the third day, she felt wonderfully alive. She had a purpose in life and nothing could take that away from her. Memories of Roarke were vivid, and everywhere. He had been across on a flying visit only recently, her father told her as they sat in the cool of the evening at the front of the house sipping long cool drinks, and he had asked after her.

'How was he?' she enquired very casually.

'Fine.' Her father nodded. 'Busy—between trips, of course. He was setting off for Tierra del Fuego after leaving us. Said to tell you he's not found a typist for his book yet, but he's still looking.' He chuckled. 'He's a grand fellow.'

'Yes,' she agreed absently, looking round, hiding her pain very successfully. Roarke had enquired politely after her. What else had she expected? A declaration of undying love? She gave a wry smile at that thought. Roarke was a happy man, doing what he wanted to do, and enjoying it. She wondered how many women he had made love to since their parting, and her nails dug into her palms and she fought for calm. None of them would matter to him anyway, any more than their lovemaking had. He had probably forgotten . . .

Her father's voice interrupted her, telling her of the screecher monkeys he had been trying to capture—making her laugh in the telling, and so forget for a while.

She stayed there for a lovely two weeks, and during the time decided where she would go next. The one place in the world where she would not go was Tierra del Fuego, but that left a lot of other areas, and she didn't really want to go to England, but wasn't sure why. It was Olivia who helped her to decide. They were sitting chatting one evening in the library, leaving the men to an interminable game of poker in the drawing room, when she asked Joanna what she intended to do when she left them.

'I want to work,' Joanna replied. 'Not at the orphanage yet—but I will go back soon. I just want a change, I suppose.' She shrugged. 'But I haven't a clue as to what kind.'

'Work? But you don't know what kind?'

'I haven't even thought yet. I just feel restless——'

'I know what you mean.' The older woman smiled wisely. 'You're still in a transition period from your old life—your father's so happy, you know. He's remarked on the change in you. He loves you very much, Joanna, and you *are* different. I can hardly believe it myself.'

'Nor can I!' Joanna laughed. 'I look in the mirror and see this creature—almost a hippy—staring back at me. My hairdresser would have a pink fit if he saw me!' She ran her fingers through her golden hair, wild and free, and shook her head. She had filled out as well—in all the right places. Too slender before, now proportioned with fuller, feminine curves that she found pleasing.

Her stepmother grinned impishly. 'Roarke wouldn't

recognise you, that's for sure!' Joanna was always startled whenever his name was mentioned out of the blue, the very name a stab of pain in her heart—and pleasure—at actually hearing the beloved word, Roarke. She looked down at the drink in her hand, and she did not see the sudden awareness that filled Olivia's eyes.

'I don't think anyone would,' she agreed, voice light.

'I do have an idea,' Olivia continued, after going to refresh their glasses. 'But whether you'd be interested or not——' she let her voice tail away, and Joanna looked up.

'You could try me.' The moment of bittersweet shock had passed. All was normal.

'Well, it would be *almost* a rest for you, after the orphanage—how do you feel about birds and animals?'

Joanna laughed. 'I think I have my father's instinctive love of most living creatures—I didn't really discover that fact till I came here—but I was most concerned about the birds when we had our—trouble with the headhunters. I didn't want to leave them. But I'll be honest, I've never looked after any. Why are you asking? You have something in mind?'

'There's an island in the Windwards which is virtually a bird sanctuary. It's inhabited by an old friend of John's, a Colonel Nesbitt—Charles Nesbitt, as mad as a hatter but an old love. And he logs turtles to see how far they travel, and where and why, etcetera.' She laughed. 'It's a paradise. No tourists, no people, only Charlie and his wife Minnie. If we ever need a break from everything, we go there. If you take a couple of bottles of best Scotch, he'll be your friend for life, and if you can recognise a few birds—and, my dear, we have enough books for you to swot up on here—you can spend a glorious few weeks there. It's lonely, it's got absolutely no entertainment, save, I must warn you, for Charlie's stereo which booms out classical musical all over the island for hours each day. Take your ear-plugs if you can't stand Tchaikovsky, otherwise relax and enjoy it. He has this theory, you see, that birds and turtles—and fish—appreciate good music. He may well be right.'

Joanna, dazed by the pictures conjured up, could only sit open-mouthed, intent. 'You're not joking, are you?' she gasped at last.

'No, my dear, I'm not. If you feel you can cope there, I'm sure he'd love to have you.'

'Good whisky,' said Joanna thoughtfully. 'Mmm, I think I'm almost on my way. Are all Dad's friends equally fascinating?'

Olivia gave a beautiful slow smile that lit her face. 'My dear, you haven't even begun to meet them yet. They are some of the most wonderful people anyone could wish to know, I promise you. He has the happy knack of gathering kindred souls around him. This house is comparatively quiet now—there are times when it's crowded to the rafters. We lead a rich, full life. I wouldn't change it for anything.'

'How odd,' Joanna mused. 'I'd always thought——' she stopped, searching for words. 'I'd always thought the life I led was the only one anybody could wish for. I didn't know a thing about living, did I?'

Olivia shook her head. 'No, Joanna, that you didn't,' she agreed softly. 'There's so much more if you know where to look. And I think you've found out where to look now. You won't want to go back to what was, ever.'

'I'd almost forgotten about it,' Joanna answered. 'I look forward to each day with a sense of adventure and wonder.' She stood up and pirouetted around on the spot. 'But I do believe that I might just take a bikini with me on *this* trip if the island is the paradise you say.' She pursed her lips. 'And I *might* take off the odd hour or two from chatting to the parakeets to actually drink in a little sun.'

Olivia shook her head in mock disapproval. 'How disgusting!' Then she grinned. 'Wish we could join you.' A pause. 'And we might. We just might.'

Joanna thought about Olivia's remarks a week or so later when she had actually settled on Paradine Island. The work—if it could be called that—was hardly arduous. Charlie and Minnie Nesbitt were a couple of colourful eccentrics, had accepted her much as they would a long-lost daughter, installed her in a beach cabin several hundred yards away from their rambling, untidy bungalow, told her to do exactly as she wished, invited her to a welcoming party in her honour—with just the three of them there—and led her gently to bed at five in the morning after a riotous evening which she could scarcely remember at all the following day, when she was aroused at noon by the rousing strains of 'Land of Hope and Glory' echoing round her cabin. She groaned, pulled the pillows over her head and turned over. It was no use at all. The brief pause when that was over was followed by a quieter but no less penetrating overture to an opera she could not at that moment recognise. Yielding to the inevitable, she staggered into her primitive shower cubicle, emerged slightly less jaded, dressed in the brief red bikini, and walked down to the sea. She waded in—and began to laugh. Gloriously uninhibited peals of laughter rang out as she swam along the shoreline. She was mad; they were mad; everyone was mad!

The insanity, if that was what it was, continued. She got used to the music, which somehow never afterwards seemed as loud as it had the first time. She enjoyed the variety of it, began to hum the more familiar opera choruses, and even to know when they were coming up on the various tapes, and spent one entire afternoon with Charlie and Minnie conducting the Hallé Orchestra in an extensive repertoire. Charlie was short and stocky, with flaming red hair and beard. He looked like a beachcomber, as did Minnie, who was taller, slimmer, with short grey curly hair and dazzling kaftans. They talked to their turtle visitors, and Joanna began to feel sure that the large gentle creatures responded both to voices and music.

One evening, sitting on the verandah of the bungalow, sipping dry Martinis and nibbling nuts, Charlie said diffidently, in his clipped Oxford accent, so at variance with his lovable tramplike appearance:

'I wonder, Joanna, if you would do Minnie and me a favour?'

'Of course. Anything.' She smiled at them both.

'Well, it's only since you arrived that we've even considered it. But Min has a sister living in Barbados—it's her silver wedding soon and they're throwing a party, you know? Well, we have our boat here, and if we could pop off for a day or two—hmm? Would you mind awfully?'

'Of course not.'

'The island can look after itself, of course. It's just nice for you to be here, in charge as it were. There's the radio—we'll keep in contact—and we'll only be away a week, what say, Min?'

'A week?' Minnie gave her husband and Joanna a sweet, misty smile. 'Oh, how lovely! I can go shopping in Bridgetown.' She sighed. 'It's so nice to have a teensy holiday now and again, Joanna.'

'I'm sure it is. And of course I'll manage. It's lovely here. I'm certainly not earning my keep. In fact I suspect Olivia only told me about you because she thought I needed a holiday. Which is precisely what I'm having.' Joanna stretched her arms above her head. 'I'm getting the most glorious tan, and swimming every day, and talking to the birds and bees. What more can anyone ask?'

'Well, me dear, that seems to be settled, then,' said Charlie, slapping his thigh. 'By jove! I must say I'm lookin' forward to this immensely.' He stood up. 'Hmm, think I'll toddle off to the boat and give it a look over. Excuse me, ladies.' He grinned at them both and vanished into the velvety darkness, humming the overture to *Lohengrin* with great gusto, and enthusiasm.

'Oh, *do* pour us another Martini, dear,' Minnie asked Joanna. 'So kind.' She beamed at her. 'We really are lucky having you here. You're so like your father. Dear John, we must have him and Olivia over soon. They love music too, you know.' She chatted on happily, no need for Joanna to reply, happy to talk, and Joanna equally happy to listen.

By the following morning it was all arranged. And the day following that, Charlie and Minnie set out on their boat, the *Lady Minnie*, and Joanna, after waving them off, wandered back to the bungalow to tidy up before lunch. After that she would sunbathe. Her day was planned. Everything on the island was perfect, even the music, which, she now realised, she would miss terribly when she left.

It was far too hot to sunbathe after lunch, and she lay instead in the shade of a cluster of palms, sleepy with the heat, and drowsier from the haunting violin concerto that was being softly played and relayed from a nearby speaker. She drifted into a half dreaming state, where reality merges into fantasy with no clear dividing line, and she was with Roarke, and the golden images blurred and sharpened inside her mind in a beautiful slow moving kaleidoscope of half remembered conversations and embraces, filling her with happiness and peace.

In her dream she saw him walking towards her from out of the sea, and sat up to watch him come nearer, blinking the sleep from her eyes so that his outline sharpened and became more clearly defined with every step that he took—only she wasn't dreaming, for the sand was gritty beneath her, and her face burned with the sun, which it never did in dreams, and she rose slowly to her feet.

'Hello,' he said, and the last shreds of what might have been a dream were there no longer. Joanna opened her mouth to answer, but no sounds came out. 'Did I wake you?'

'Roarke!' She wanted to run and hold him, to hug him, to blend with him and be part of him—but she stayed where she was, looking, just looking at him, then, as he reached her, held out her hand. 'Hello, Roarke,' she said. 'It *is* you. I thought I was dreaming——'

He was looking at her as though he had never seen her before. 'My God,' he said softly. 'It *is* Joanna, isn't it? You're so—different.'

'Mmm, aren't I?' she laughed. 'Come and have a drink, and we'll talk.'

She didn't know why he had come. She only knew that he was the man she wanted to see most in all the world, and her wish had come true. She took his arm and led him towards the bungalow.

# CHAPTER TEN

'WHERE are Minnie and Charlie?' Roarke asked, as she returned with two long iced drinks.

'Gone to Barbados for a few days. No need to ask if you know them.' She sat down in a cane chair.

'Doesn't everybody?' he laughed. 'But I didn't expect to see you here. I thought you'd be back in England, or somewhere in Europe by now.'

His words, casually said, let her know several things. He had not come to see her, but his old friends. The thought at the back of her mind, by nothing he said, but left unsaid, was that he wouldn't have bothered if he had known—which might be unfair, but she was sensitive to every subtle shade of meaning with Roarke. They also let her know, by casual implication, that his lack of interest in her was total. He thought she would have been somewhere in Europe by now. He was therefore mildly surprised to see her, but no more than that. And if I did have any illusions, she thought, they would have gone by now.

'No, I'm having a break. How in the world did you get here? I don't see your helicopter.'

'I borrowed a friend's cabin cruiser for a few days, having a jaunt round the islands calling on old pals.' He nodded his head. 'I'm moored in an inlet not far away.'

'No expeditions to deepest Peru?' She paused fractionally before the last word, about to have said Tierra del Fuego, but that might seem as though she knew all about his movements, which would never do. She would not only match him for casualness, she would surpass him.

'No. I have holidays too, occasionally.'

159

'And catch up on your writing?' She was quite surprising herself by her polite indifference.

'I might. Why not?'

'And haven't you found a publisher yet?' she teased.

'I haven't even found a typist—I told your father to tell you.'

Joanna frowned as if trying to remember. 'Ah—perhaps he *did* mention something.' A masterpiece of understatement. She had treasured that little gem along with other memories, but the delicate verbal fencing match was under way. 'What a shame. Still, you will, one day, I'm sure.'

One part of her seemed to be standing back listening to the conversation. They were like two strangers who, thrown together by chance, and having absolutely no interest in each other, make small talk to pass the time. The contrast between their other enforced proximity could hardly have been greater. Virtually housebound in the middle of the jungle, while here they were surrounded by sea, on an island that held a profusion of exotic flowers and trees, free to wander about, to swim, to sunbathe. One thing remained the same. They were completely alone.

Last time she had been his virtual prisoner, abducted by him; this time they met on equal terms. Both free, both there by choice—and she, changed beyond recognition by all that had happened to her. Physically, not only mentally, she was a different woman. She watched him over the rim of her glass. Roarke too looked different to the eyes of love with which she saw him. It was months since they had parted. He was slightly thinner, almost as though he might have been ill. There was a faint scar on his temple, last legacy of their few days together in Amazonia, and his tan was deeper, his hair slightly longer—only his eyes were the same. The eyes that had once looked at her with desire and longing were as hard as she had ever known them at the beginning. She sensed the gulf that lay between them, and accepted it. There was no way it would ever be bridged, but she loved him enough to accept that it was there, and not to mind. He had changed her, had made her the woman she was now, and for this she owed him everything.

He would never love her in return, never love any woman, if Olivia was correct—and she usually was—but at least he was here, now, with her, and that was richness beyond counting. Joanna sighed. 'I'm glad you've come,' she said. 'I don't know how long you're here for, but feel free to relax and enjoy yourself in the time you have—let me look after you.' It was said almost impishly, and she saw his eyebrows go up in mild surprise.

'That's an offer I can't refuse,' he remarked.

'It's the least I can do. It was, after all, you who made me see things differently, and I don't forget that. I'll prove to you I'm not the woman I was when we met. I'll even—and this is a sacrifice above and beyond human endeavour—type out some more for you on Charlie's extremely grotty typewriter, and when you've seen it you'll appreciate why I use the word sacrifice—if you want to stay a day or so.'

Roarke hung his head, apparently overwhelmed. 'Too much,' he murmured. 'What can I say?' When he lifted his head, he was laughing. 'I *have* seen Charlie's typewriter. It should have been consigned to the deep years ago.' He lifted his hand. 'But—wait for it—guess what I have on board my boat?'

'The mind boggles,' she murmured. 'Pray tell.'

'A new, portable de-luxe typewriter, with—wait for it again—a box of paper and a pad of carbons.'

'Good *heavens*!'

'Your noble efforts put me to shame. If I can't learn to press keys I'm not the man I think I am, I thought, so I bought a typewriter and all the necessary bits and pieces and decided to teach myself.'

'And have you?'

'Not yet.' He pulled a face. 'Give me time.'

'There's no time like the present. I've got nothing to do this evening. No turtles to talk to—or if there are they can wait—and the birds hereabouts are pretty self-sufficient. So—go and fetch it.'

He stretched. 'I fancy a swim first.'

'Then have one.'

'Aren't you coming too?'

Joanna shook her head. 'No, I'll get something for us to eat. You'll stay overnight?'

'As you've so kindly invited me, yes.' He stood up. The sun bronzed him, catching his hair with glints of gold. He peeled off his tee-shirt casually and threw it over the chair, then unzipped his jeans. Joanna caught her breath for a moment, then realised that he was wearing black swimming trunks and breathed again.

'Sure you won't have a swim?' he asked as he turned away.

'Perhaps later. Watch out for sharks. They don't come in too close, but there's the occasional basker.'

'I'll remember that.' He was striding away as he answered, and she watched him go, hungry to store each precious image in her mind. Roarke walked tall, head proud, shoulders broad and muscular, long back; hard, long, very muscular legs. She knew, she had touched and known every inch of that body, and she was warm with the memories. If he wanted her again he would be disappointed, because she knew now that while to her it would be an act of pure love, to him it would be merely a physical hunger satisfied. She would not take him on those terms. For her own innate self-respect, she could not. Despite her longing for him that was a knowledge deep within her, and it was a sure and certain knowledge. It added to her own inner sense of rightness. She had spoken the truth. She would look after him while he remained on the island, would feed him, type for him, prepare long cool drinks for him. But she would not touch him or allow him to touch her, and she suspected that he was as aware of it as though she had said it. Everything she did, would be done with love. And even her decision was a sacrifice to love. He would never know that.

She watched him strike out from shore, yielding to the breakers, diving and rolling, being submerged in the restless pounding sea, then she smiled and went in to find something interesting for them to eat later.

He lay in the sun, stretched out, drying off after his swim, and she crept out and sat beside him and handed him a drink of lime juice, well iced. Grains of sand covered his skin where he had rolled over before, and he sat up, brushing them from him, and took the glass from Joanna.

'You know,' he confessed, 'I could get to like this. Thanks,' he sipped. 'Mmm.'

'I told you, I'll spoil you while you're here. Make the most of it while it lasts. You can sleep in the main bungalow tonight, unless of course you prefer to sleep aboard your boat. I have a small guest cabin——' she pointed, 'along there.' It established the situation in the gentlest possible way. 'Charlie and Minnie have one spare bedroom. Apparently they've occasionally had a dozen or so guests, but everyone just sleeps outside.'

'I might do that as well. I'm used to it.'

She shrugged. 'Fine. There's an air bed somewhere.'

'What happened to the music?' asked Roarke.

She pulled a face. 'I switched it off, before you came, just for a change. Do you want it back on again?'

He laughed. 'I can live without it.'

'That's what I thought. I was woken up on my first morning here by "Land of Hope and Glory". Now *that* was an experience, I can tell you!'

'What happened?'

She told him, embroidering the facts slightly, and he listened, and it really was so casual and pleasant that they might have been two strangers learning to get on well with each other instead of a man and a woman who had shared the deepest experiences that it is possible for two people to share.

They ate together later, fish and salad—the plump ripe tomatoes grown by Minnie in her own tropical vegetable plot. She possessed the greenest of green fingers, and had proudly told Joanna that she could make almost anything grow anywhere—and it was perfectly true. Afterwards they went aboard Roarke's boat where he found typewriter and papers, and carried them back to the bungalow.

In the brief dusk before nightfall they set everything up on the verandah and placed the lamp at the correct angle for work. The only disadvantage was the moths it attracted, but Joanna was used to them now, and scarcely noticed any more.

She had been aware since their meal that the atmosphere was subtly changing, but put it down to the darkness and the fact of their being entirely alone. There was certainly nothing that she could do about it, and it wasn't even anything definite, just a faint amorphous shifting of balance. Roarke's manners and behaviour were as impeccable as ever—she realised that it might be she who was causing the shift, but was helpless to do anything about it.

She had changed earlier into a long chiffon dress of blazing orange. It swirled when she moved, and it was cool and comfortable, sleeveless, high-necked—utterly respectable. Roarke wore jeans and a white long-sleeved shirt. In the glow from the lamp on the table they looked, Joanna thought, like one of those advertisements on television for after-dinner mints, or some new liqueur—she began to laugh, and when he asked why, told him. 'Hmm,' he agreed. 'You might have something there. Only trouble is—shouldn't I be wearing a bow tie?'

'With jeans?' she spluttered.

He got up, without a word, and disappeared into the darkness. For a foolish moment Joanna assumed that she had offended him by her laughter, and wondered where he had gone. She hadn't long to wait to find out.

There was a loud cough from the darkness, the kind that announces the arrival of someone new on the scene, and she turned to see him come into the light—and he had changed. He wore jeans no longer, but dark evening trousers, dazzling shirt, and black bow tie. A jacket was slung casually over his arm. The difference in his appearance was startling. He laid the jacket over the back of his chair and said with a grin: 'It's too darned warm for that yet. All right? This do you?'

'How very civilised! I approve.'

'Thank you, ma'am,' he drawled, and sat down. 'Now, how about a liqueur with our coffee? We might as well go the whole hog and Charlie usually has some Benedictine in that wine cellar of his.' As she made to get up, he stood. 'Stay right where you are. My turn.'

Then he was gone. Joanna remained seated, thoughtful. He had a sense of humour and timing that she fully appreciated; subtle and dry. She gazed into the outer darkness, the sea faintly lit with a new moon, palms outlined in feathery black shapes that moved fractionally in a slight breeze, and with them, around them, the never ending chirk-chirk of night insects in trees and shrubs. It was a night for love and lovers, a perfect place for anyone to be, the air sweet scented and soft and warm, and she would remember this moment for always and ever in the secret place in her heart that she would keep for him. She waited now for him to return, as the gentle breeze touched her cheeks and neck and stirred her hair with featherlight caress. She wanted him very much. She wanted him so much that it was a deep pain inside her, and when he came out bearing a tray with coffee and liqueurs on she had to fight back the overwhelming torment and put on a pleasant smile, and thank him, and ask him some inane question about typing because she didn't know what else to say.

'Why don't you teach me?' he asked.

'Now?'

'Why not?'

'Why not indeed?' she returned lightly, and made him sit at the table, then stood behind him, leaning over so that their bodies were touching, and her hair brushed the back of his neck. She put his hands on the keys, positioning his fingers correctly, and said: 'That's how you begin. See?'

'Mmm,' he nodded, and she could smell the faint scent of after shave, and the clean salty tang of his sea-washed hair. But he was busy concentrating on the keyboard and she might have been a sexless creature dressed in a potato sack for all the notice he took of her nearness. Which was entirely as it should be, and she was grateful. 'So? What next?'

'You practise, idiot,' she answered shakily. 'You do this—and this——' she moved his hands off, leaned over and demonstrated the fingering techniques, a to q and back, s to w, d to e—repeating them over and over until——

'Ah!' A great light dawned. 'Ah, yes, I see.'

She stood back and applauded, a slow clapping of her hands. 'Hurray, he's got it! By George, I think he's got it!'

Roarke whirled round and out of his chair and stood up suddenly, towering over her, and caught her arms. 'You're mocking me,' he growled. 'Mocking a defenceless man!' but he released her as he spoke because the shudder that she had given was quite beyond her control, and he knew—he knew. Then it suddenly wasn't all right any more. It was suddenly and devastatingly all wrong. And both knew, and neither could speak or say or move.

Joanna was first to break the growing, unbearable tension. 'The-then you have to keep p-practising,' she stammered. 'It's not easy——'

'No, I shouldn't imagine it is,' he spoke quickly as though trying to save her from something not definable. 'And of course daylight is a better time—stupid really to try now.'

'Yes. My coffee—it will be getting cold.' She picked up her cup and moved away. The tension crackled all around them and she held on to her cup with both hands, like a child learning to drink from one, and looked wide-eyed at the table and searched for something to say. Her heart hammered in her breast.

Roarke fumbled in his pocket. 'Mind if I smoke?'

'No, not at all.'

'Damn, I can't find my lighter——'

'There's one inside on the table.'

'Thanks.' He vanished and she managed to breathe. What was happening? Nothing was happening, nothing had happened, and nothing would, but the air was almost raw, almost crackling with electricity. She didn't want to sit or stand. She didn't know what she wanted to do.

He emerged, puffing at a cigar as though his life depended on it.

'That's better. Found it all right.' He pulled at his tie. 'God, it's hot.'

'Is it?' That was stupid. 'Of course it is. It'll cool down later.'

'I hope so. Coffee all right?'

'Yes, fine. Look, if you want to turn in, Roarke, I'll——' she cleared her throat. 'I'll go to bed——'

'No. No. I was thinking of going for a last swim to cool down.'

'Oh, nice.' She wished her stupid heart would slow down a bit.

'But you're not going to?'

'Er—no.'

'Ah.'

'In fact, I'm rather tired,' she said, and yawned. 'I think I'll just have a shower tonight and get to bed.' A cold shower, as cold as possible, she thought.

'I won't make a noise.'

'No. Well, I'll——' she finished the sweet liqueur and put her glass down. 'I'll say goodnight, then, Roarke.'

'Yes. Goodnight, Joanna.'

She turned and walked away across the sand towards her cabin. Inside she locked the door, pulled down the blinds, and walked across to her shower room.

She spent the next two hours trying desperately and vainly to get to sleep.

When she awoke from a restless dream it was still cool and dark outside, but she was boiling. She lay for a few minutes on her side, coming to life again, surfacing unwillingly to the realisation that she had to face Roarke later. It was not as simple and wonderful as she had at first thought. His very presence was disturbing, his nearness, as over the typewriter at his lesson, far more so. That was the reason she had declined to go swimming, but she wondered how much longer she could go on coping with the situation. She loved him and she wanted him. That was quite simple. He did not love her. He might want her, might desire to take her, casually and calmly, before he departed, but that wasn't so simple. She would despise herself, knowing that to him it would be nothing.

'Damn, damn, *damn*!' she exclaimed, stubbing her toe on the leg of the bed and hopping to the shower. Half way there she stopped. Why not a swim now, while he was asleep?

She slung her nightdress off, donned her bikini, and very quietly unlocked her door.

All was quiet outside, even the sea hushed and smooth, and the air was sufficiently cool to make her shiver slightly as she tiptoed down to the water. She could see the huddled shape in front of the bungalow. He lay on an air bed with a blanket over him, and made not a sound. Joanna ran into the water and dived forward, gasping with the mild shock as the sea covered her. She swam lazily about, keeping always within a safe distance of shore, floated on her back watching the sky lighten almost visibly, stars vanishing as though they had never been. Soon the sun would rise, a burnished red disc appearing first as a thin line, growing and rising and becoming brighter and rounder until it burst into full glorious life, and the day would have begun. That was some time off yet.

Her hair floated round her as she lay on her back, soothed by the warm salty caress of the sea on her limbs, and she kicked out, splashing, propelling herself backward just enough to keep from sinking.

It was all right, of course it was. Roarke wasn't aware of her feelings. Last night had been her imagination. It had been a pleasant, amusing evening and she was quite sure he had enjoyed it as much as she had. Her imagination was too vivid, that was all. She saw things that weren't there. I'm a silly idiot, she told herself. Enjoy this day, make the most of what time there is before he leaves, and accept. Just accept.

It seemed to make everything easier, thinking along those lines, and she was about to go ashore when she heard Roarke's voice hailing her, and she flipped over in the water to wave to him.

'What's it like?' he shouted.

'Fine. Come on in.'

'Give me one minute.' She turned and swam away at slow pace. She would have another five minutes with him and then go out. That was a simple enough decision to make. She heard movement and turned, and he was swimming towards her.

'I was just about to come out,' she said.

'You should have woken me before.'

'You were fast asleep. I couldn't do that.' They swam side by side, at a leisured pace, neither trying to race, parallel to the shore, and rounded the island to see his boat moored peacefully in the inlet, bobbing slightly with the movement of the water.

'Come aboard, let's have a drink,' he suggested.

'All right. Why not?'

He climbed the fixed ladder first and reached down to help her over. Joanna stood shivering on deck. 'Brrh! It's cold when you get out.'

He led the way down to his cabin. 'Grab a towel—here——' he flung her a large brown one. 'Get dry.' He crouched by the fridge and brought out two cans of beer. 'All I have, sorry. Not too early, I hope?'

'Terribly, but never mind.' She slung the towel round her shoulders and sat down on the vinyl-covered bench seat that would open into a bed. The boat was compact but comfortable. She bounced experimentally on the seat. 'Mmm, nice.'

'Want a little trip?' asked Roarke.

'Where to?'

'Anywhere. Next island if you like. Pick some fruit.'

'Okay.' She opened her beer and poured it into the glass he handed to her. 'Cheers.'

'Cheers.' He drank his in one. 'Come up on deck when you're ready. We'll watch the sun rise very soon.'

She nodded and watched him go. The beer, on an empty stomach, had a pleasantly dizzying effect. She rubbed herself dry on the towel, emptied her glass, and ran up to the deck. As she did so he started the motors and she held on to the rail as the boat turned slowly round, then she went to join him at the wheel. She stood beside him as he steered the cruiser out towards open water, and the breeze was in her face and blowing her hair about.

'Want a go at steering?' he shouted above the engine roar.

'Yes, please!' she yelled back, and he moved her in and stood behind her, placing her hands on the wheel and leaving his resting lightly on top. The sensation was glorious. The powerful engines throbbed beneath their feet, and they stood closely together, legs braced against overbalance, and his body lined hers like a warm cloak and she knew the headiness of his physical nearness, and, aching, stirred fractionally, scarcely aware of what she was doing, only knowing that she wanted to stay like this for ever.

'Okay?' he asked, but not shouting, this time he whispered it in her ear so that his breath tickled her, and a shiver ran through her.

'Yes, it's lovely.' He meant the steering, she meant something entirely different, and she was being quite, quite reckless, and she didn't care any more. She half turned to tell him, she thought she intended, that the beer had made her slightly dizzy and she hoped that it wouldn't affect her judgment in steering, and she opened her mouth to speak and he had his head very close; he hadn't moved away, he was still bending over her and she shouldn't have turned back, because her face touched his face and she felt his rough bristles scrape her cheeks and exclaimed: 'Ouch!' and he said huskily:

'What is it?'

'Silly of me—I—was just going to say—only your b-beard——'

'Careful,' he said, 'you're sway——'

Her mouth, tremulous and trembling, touched his.

She felt rather than heard the engines putter away into silence, but it was as from a distance. Her mind and body exploded with the intensity of the kiss for which she had been waiting ever since he had walked towards her on the beach. Their bodies were on fire with mutual heat as they clung together, lost in a world far away from any reality. Endless moments blended and the kiss became deeper, more intense, so perfect that she thought she would die if it went on, so wonderful that she had never known anything like it.

Movement and sound blurred, and she felt the softness beneath her body, heard heartbeats so loud, not sure whether hers or his, felt his arms and legs twining round her. She was only vaguely aware of having been carried, only faintly conscious of anything save the immediate urgency of the moment as Roarke touched her and kissed her with those familiar hands and mouth that she knew only too dangerously well. She revelled again in the preliminaries to his lovemaking, yearning with her body fully alive and finely attuned to his every need and desire, then the sun rose in a glorious burst of colour, flooding the cabin with light and fire and brilliant golds. A beam touched her eyes and forehead in a blaze of flame and she jerked her face away—and she realised then what was about to happen, and it was nearly too late.

'No——' she struggled, pushing him, and he, nearly lost, nearly beyond stopping, lay on his side, stunned with shock, then reached for her again. 'No,' she repeated, and it was all over, because he took his hands away from her and sat in a huddled crouch beside her on the bunk bed, head bent, hands to face, shattered. Joanna took a deep, shuddering breath. She had not intended this to happen—or had she? She didn't know. All she knew was that however much she wanted him she had to deny her own desires, or she would never be free.

'I'm sorry, Roarke,' she said. She was prepared for

his anger, his bitterness—she braced herself for the whip-lash——

'Don't,' he said. 'It's I who should——' He stopped. He was making efforts to recover, breathing deeply, clenching and unclenching his hands as if it would help him regain control more quickly.

For a few moments after that there were no words spoken, none needed. The air still crackled with terrible tension, but neither moved. Then Roarke lifted his head. 'That was stupid,' he said. 'Oh, God, but that was so *stupid.*' He crashed his fist down on the edge of the bunk as if wanting to hurt himself. The wood splintered with the force of the blow, which rocked them both, but it served to break the intolerable emotions that swirled round them, filling the small cabin, making Joanna tremble. She stood up and moved away, rubbing her arms briskly as if to restore the circulation.

'I'd better—I think I'll go——' she began. She realised, belatedly, that her bikini strap was half way down her arm, and hitched it up.

'Wait. Not yet. Make coffee—black. I need——' He stood up as well. 'I'll make——'

'No, sit down. I'll——' She swallowed. Nearness was danger. The cabin was small. 'Please, Roarke, I'll do it.'

He knew as well. He sat down, and Joanna cleared her throat. 'You can tell me where everything is. W-when we get back I'll type for you—on the beach——'

'Yes. Coffee in that cupboard——'

'Oh. Ah, yes.' The kettle was filled with great care and precision by Joanna, who found comfort in action. She lit the gas, placed the kettle on, found the coffee, cups and spoons—found, too, that a calmness was replacing what had passed. She did not look at him, nor he at her. Both wore an invisible protective covering that kept them apart. She handed him his coffee and he thanked her with grave courtesy, careful not to touch her hand as she passed the cup to him. She still found his mood surprising. Anger would have been natural, this was not. It showed her yet another side to him that she could not possibly have guessed at. Anger, a sharp, bitter exchange, would have been therapeutic in a way. Instead this serious man, so hard, tough as steel, was behaving as if he were the one at fault. She knew he wasn't. Whatever had so nearly happened had been because she had wanted him. She wanted to tell him that, but she could not speak. She could only drink her coffee, hot strong and bitter, and hold her aching hurt inside her where it didn't show.

'We must talk,' he said at last, and she sensed the effort it was for him to say the words.

'No, I'd rather not——' she began, and he cut in:

'Yes. Don't you see? We must.'

'It won't happen again.' She was able to look at him now for the first time, and saw that he hurt too, that his pain was possibly greater than hers.

'How the hell do we know that?'

'Because it won't.' Agitated anew, she stood up and moved away. 'We'll have to—not get close, that's all—and you must go.' The last words were wrenched out of her.

'I'm not leaving you here alone,' he said flatly. 'I can't.'

'I was prepared to be alone. I have a radio——'

'That's not the point. I'm staying until they get back.'

'I don't *want* you here.'

His head jerked back as though with shock. Then he took a deep breath. 'That doesn't make any difference,' he said harshly. 'I'll take us back to the island now. Stay and finish your coffee down here.' He stood up, but he couldn't pass her unless he came too close, and he remained standing where he was. So did Joanna. He would have to ask her to move.

'I didn't ask you to come,' she said. 'I was happy alone——' She put her cup down on the table. 'I'm not a child, Roarke.'

'I know that only too well.' There was no anger in him. There should have been. She, conversely, felt her temper welling up, a mixture of love and hate mingling in a terrifying combination that she neither understood nor could control.

'Because you've made love to me before, that's why, isn't it?' she asked, voice rising. 'Oh, yes, you know only too well! That's what you wanted when you brought me aboard—answer me, damn you!'

'There's no point,' he said in level tones. 'You want a fight, I don't. I'm not going to fight you any more——'

'Lost your courage?' she taunted, and took a step towards him. 'What the hell are you? Tell me that——'

'There's no point in this. Will you let me pass——' he began.

'No, damn you, I won't! You wanted to talk. Well, talk. Tell me what you wanted to say. Go on. Were you going to apologise for nearly making love to me?' She began to laugh, mocking him, hating him, and frightened by what she was doing, and hurting inside, and yet unable to stop—'You're not a man!' she gasped. 'Do you hear me? You're not a man——' He moved swiftly, lifted her to one side and went past her. Almost hysterical, she grabbed hold of his arm and jerked him round. 'Don't touch me,' she sobbed. 'How *dare* you touch me——' and she lashed out at him and caught him a blow on his shoulder that rocked him. He looked at her, then walked out and away from her. His eyes held an agony that was unbearable.

# CHAPTER ELEVEN

JOANNA collapsed on to the bunk and rolled over into a small bundle of crying misery. She felt the deep shudder of the engines as they started up, but was almost oblivious to what was happening. What had happened? She had lashed out at Roarke in anger and bitterness—seeking, she now knew, a fight—and he had not retaliated in any way, merely looked at her, and gone. She lay there, body burning, and cried hot, angry tears, but the anger was with herself. She loved him deeply, and she had wanted to hurt him.

The sobbing gradually died away and she sat up, then rinsed her face at the sink, and thought herself into calm, for when they would reach home. They were nearly there now. The boat was slowing, edging its way into the inlet, and she washed the empty cups, then went slowly up on deck, her heart sad.

Roarke was switching off engines. She waited on deck for him to leave the controls, and watched him walk towards her. 'I'm truly sorry, Roarke,' she said. 'I don't know what came over me.'

He gave a very faint grin, but it said more than words could. 'Let's try and forget it, shall we?' He looked deeply into her eyes. 'Let's begin at the beginning. We haven't been for a trip on the boat. We went for a swim, and now we're returning for breakfast, and perhaps some work? Okay?'

She shook her head. 'I don't understand you. You're—different.'

'We're both different people from the ones who met at a party in Manaos. And we both know it, accept it.'

'I am. At least—correction—I thought I was, until I lost control just now. But you—you don't need to change.'

'Don't I?' Roarke swung his leg over the side and began to climb down. Joanna, after a pause to let him land, followed suit. He didn't offer to help her ashore, but he waited for her. They walked along the hot sunny beach side by side, a foot or more apart, and neither spoke for several minutes. She felt helplessly confused by him and by all that had happened. She still wanted him, that was the awful thing, and she sensed that he wanted her equally. The fact lay unspoken between them like a kind of electric current that could not be switched off but would always be there.

And he wasn't leaving; he had made that very clear. She didn't want him to leave, although she had said so in her anger and despair. He would stay until the Nesbitts' return, that was definite. How would she bear it?

She slung herself on the sand near his makeshift bed. 'I'm not hungry,' she said.

'Nor am I.' He sat down, not too near.

'So I'll type.'

'You will?'

'Yes. Work is good for one, I've discovered.'

'And you've been doing quite a bit of that since we last met, haven't you?'

'You mean at the orphanage? Did Olivia tell you?'

'Yes.'

'I enjoyed it. It was hard work, but I discovered I liked doing it. I'm going back there soon.'

'And you surprised yourself?'

'Yes.' She looked at him. 'I did. You changed me. You—and Father, of course.' She lay back on the sand. 'Damn, I'll have to wash my hair. It's all sticky with sea water.'

'I changed you? How?'

She shrugged. Where did she begin to answer a question like that? 'Oh, you already know. You made me see things differently.' That was casual—and safe— enough for anyone.

'Mmm, thanks. You were ready for change. I just happened along at the right moment, that's all.'

'Perhaps.' She rolled over on to her stomach. She could see him better now, sitting there propped on one elbow, looking at her. That was all, just looking. Nothing wrong with that. All was well, comparatively calm, desire abated. Under control. It was there, it always would be there, but she would have to learn to live with that. She didn't only love him, she liked him as a person, for everything he was. She would suffer the desires of her treacherous body and just accept that he was there and make the most of every moment with him, treasures to be stored up for the future when she could take them out, these precious memories, and savour them. She reached across impulsively and touched his arm. If she had thought about it, she would not have done it, but she didn't think. It was almost as though her arm moved of its own volition. 'I'm sorry I hit you, and I'm sorry I said I wanted you to go. I don't. We'll go back to what I said last night. I'll look after you while you're here. All right?'

He looked down at her hand, and she took it away, casually, slowly, then lay down flat on her stomach, her face turned towards him, supported by her arms. I love you, I love you, she said silently, in her head, then closed her eyes lest they should tell him what her mouth did not.

He gave a deep sigh. 'Oh, Joanna, you'll spoil me.'

'I know! Relax and enjoy it.'

'It's an offer I can't refuse. Typing as well! Too much.'

'I shall expect the occasional cold drink while I'm working, of course,' she said, voice muffled now that at last she was beginning to relax.

'Of course!'

She was tired. The night's restless sleep was taking its toll, and she yawned. Minutes passed, and she felt herself beginning to doze off and tried to resist it, but grew drowsier still. She opened her eyes briefly at a slight sound, and Roarke too was lying down, on his side, facing her. He had closed his eyes. That was the last thing she saw before she fell asleep.

When she awoke it was to find herself covered entirely in a thin sheet. Roarke had disappeared. She sat up, pulling the sheet away, and heard his voice from the verandah. 'I didn't want you to get sunstroke. The sun's very hot.'

'How long have I slept?' She rubbed her eyes, then scrambled to her feet.

'Only an hour.' She walked towards him and sat on a chair beside him in the shade.

'Oh, I feel better. Did you sleep too?'

'Only for a few minutes. Then I had a shower and changed.' He wore faded denim shorts with ragged edges at the thighs.

Joanna stretched herself. 'I shall do the same,' she announced, 'then we'll eat.'

'It's all ready, waiting in the fridge, salad and fruit and smoked salmon.'

'Good gracious! I thought I was the chef.'

'Later. Go and get your shower. I'll practise my typing.' He flexed his fingers and studied them thoughtfully. 'Hmm, no problem. Just half an hour and I'll be perfect.'

She snorted her disbelief and walked smartly off towards her cabin, laughing. When she emerged he was indeed practising, but with much muttered swearing. 'Perfect yet?' she enquired gently, standing behind him. His only answer was a deep, explosive sigh.

'Stupid bloody machine,' he muttered, and turned to glare at her.

She laughed. 'Temper! Move over and let an expert

get to work. Where are your notes?'

'Here.' He moved aside for her. 'Just a few. I don't want a sudden breeze to blow everything away.' He used a large flat stone as paperweight and put them on the table. 'I'll get our salad first.'

Joanna sat down, ripped out the paper containing his clumsy, oddly spaced efforts, and put it to one side. When he came out bearing two plates, she was ready to begin, paper in machine, notes in order, erasing strip in position in case of errors.

They ate in pleasant silence interrupted only by casual remarks that needed no answers, or little thought. When they had finished, Joanna set to work and became oblivious to the passage of time. She was aware that Roarke had disappeared without a word, but saw him returning a short time afterwards carrying boxes. He came from the direction of his boat.

'Want a drink?' he called, as he passed.

'Please. What have you brought?'

'Food from the boat. I contacted Charlie and Min before, while you were asleep, and told them I was here. They're staying in Barbados for another week—or more.'

He dropped the last two words in as though they had no significance, but she felt herself stiffen. She stared at what she had just typed, but the words suddenly made no sense. Why? Why? The question hammered in her head.

'Joanna? What is it?'

She jerked her head up. 'Nothing, I was just re-reading what I'd typed——' she smiled. He watched her, and she looked away again. He saw too much.

'They haven't had a holiday for a while. They're happy that I'm here—they wouldn't have left you alone that long, but now——' he shrugged. 'They send their love, by the way.'

'Oh. That's nice.' She watched him go in. There was something that was making her uneasy; not just the fact of them being alone for at least another week, not that. Something more, something not right, that she didn't understand at all. She simply did not understand what was happening. It was all too—pat. She stood up, turned and walked down towards the sea. She had changed into shorts and tee-shirt previously, and it would not matter if they got wet, they would dry in no time at all. She needed to think, and to do so she had to be alone. She waded in, leg-deep, thigh-deep, waist-deep, and the water was warm. Soon night would fall and she would type by lamplight; the evening would pass, and they would go to their separate beds and sleep. And the pattern would continue for days and days. Roarke knew, surely, that it would be a strain? She lay back and floated, feeling the soft slap of the salty water on her body. The sun dazzled and she drifted with closed eyes, and marvelled that they should have all that time together. Of course she wanted him to stay. She wanted him to stay for ever and never go away. She wanted to be married to him, living in remote seclusion on an island such as this, with all the time in the world to make love, to swim, to hold each other close. She wanted to have his child, to carry his baby inside her. She wanted them to be together for evermore. And while he was here, in the magic time they had remaining, she would dream her dreams and pretend it was so.

The sun burned through her flimsy tee-shirt, and she turned and swam, then she heard his voice from a long way away—too long a way—calling her name. When she lifted her head it was to see, with a sense of shock, that she had come out much farther than she had before. The bungalow was a small matchbox-sized edifice— and Roarke was a dot. She began to swim towards shore, cursing herself for her stupidity, and saw, before she dived her head down to crawl, that he was running down the beach. Coming to meet her? Her lover was coming to meet her.

She swam swiftly and strongly, no fear of sea or currents within her. She was an excellent swimmer. She risked a look back, but no telltale fin followed her. There were no sharks about, which was a great relief.

Nearer and nearer the shore, the bungalow growing larger, Roarke approaching, how sweet he was to meet her—and when he was nearer she trod water and shouted: 'Hey, it was a good job you called me——'

He reached her. 'You stupid, arrogant *bitch*!' he shouted, and he was so furiously angry, livid with it, that Joanna, startled, began to laugh.

'What!' she exclaimed, and dived after him as he turned. He didn't allow her to catch up with him, and piqued, she put on a spurt of speed that should have guaranteed her passing him—only it didn't. He was ahead of her all the way, and as they waded out, she caught him up, grabbed his arm and said: '*What* did you call me?' Still half laughing because of *course* he must be joking. He wasn't really angry, he couldn't be. He hadn't been angry that morning when he could well have been, and this, in comparison, was nothing.

He whirled round and jerked his arm free of her. 'You stupid, idiotic bitch,' he said, and there was no humour either in his voice or in his face. He was angrier than she had ever seen him before, angrier than she had ever seen anyone.

Joanna was rocked back on her heels at the sheer force of his words. 'What the hell do you mean?' she gasped.

'What the hell do you think I mean?' He glared down at her, eyes blazing, almost black with his rage. 'You go near enough a mile out in shark-infested water——'

'I didn't know! I was floating——' and fantasising about marriage and babies, she thought. So much for fantasy. This man looked mad enough to hit her, and his next words confirmed it.

'I could beat you!' he grated, and stalked away from her as if he might do just that if he stayed. She caught up with him, hit him hard across the back, and when he turned, gave him a swift and resounding slap across his face.

'Then why don't you try!' she shouted, all the pent-up frustration boiling over in a temper that surpassed his. She quivered with rage, she stood facing him, incensed, ready for anything he might do—almost hoping he would—knowing that in sheer physical violence she would find some kind of release from the pressure that was building up so inexorably.

'Because I wouldn't know when to stop,' he snapped, voice harder than she had ever known, 'and don't hit me again——'

She silenced him by doing precisely that, striking him a blow that nearly rocked him. He grabbed her arm and pulled her towards him, and she kicked out and lashed out with her free arm, whirling round, back to him, her body revelling in the action she had been too long denied. She hated him, she really hated him at that moment.

He flung her from him. 'Don't touch me,' he said harshly, 'or by God I'll make you wish you hadn't.'

'I don't *care*! I hate you, do you hear? I *hate* you——'

'Shut up!'

'I wish there had been sharks,' she sobbed. 'They're preferable to you——'

'I said—shut up. You've said enough.'

'I haven't damned well begun, you bad-tempered swine! I wish I were a man, I'd give you something to think about, you absolute——'

'Don't talk so stupid.' He turned on his heel as if weary of her and strode away towards the bungalow. Joanna, exhausted and shattered, stood trembling where he had left her. She swayed slightly with sudden reaction to what had happened. In moments anger had flared, from nothing to a blazing rage, with a suddenness that frightened her. If this was how they could behave towards each other over something as relatively unimportant as swimming too far out—and she had never been in any danger—what potential was there for real, no holds barred violence? Joanna, walking slowly, went back towards the verandah, and Roarke had gone inside. She didn't want to see him, or talk to him, or look at him, not for a long time. Her nerve ends were raw with fear and tension and the terrible aftermath of their mutual destruction.

It could not go on. She sank slowly into the chair by the table and stared unseeingly at the typewriter. She was no longer angry; she was, instead, completely drained. She wasn't going to cry, but she didn't want him to come out.

If she began work, he might ignore her. If his terrible rage had evaporated slightly, all would be all right. If he was still toweringly angry she would simply go to her cabin and stay there. The choice was simple, the decision, once made, the obvious one.

When it happened, she was given no choice. She heard a door slam at the back of the bungalow, then there was silence. She waited, then, when he still had not reappeared, began typing again. An hour or so later she went in for a drink, and the bungalow was empty.

She walked quickly to where his boat was moored—only it wasn't. It had gone. He had left without a word. A sense of such utter desolation and loneliness filled her that it was almost unbearable. She put her hand to her mouth. Roarke had gone.

She ran back to the house and the emptiness washed around her, and the island had become a silent, lonely place. She sat down and looked out towards the sea, her heart breaking. 'Oh, Roarke,' she whispered, 'forgive me. I didn't mean it. I hurt, and because I hurt, I hurt you as well——'

But no one heard her. There was no one to answer her. There was something she could do. She could finish the work she had begun for him, and when she left, see that her father got it to give to Roarke. It would be something to make amends, not much, but something.

She set to with renewed energy and a sense of purpose, and she was so engrossed and stimulated by the sheer hard work of it that time passed surprisingly swiftly.

It grew dark and she lit the lamp and continued, and even though her back, arms, and eyes ached, she did not stop. She was thus engaged when she heard sounds and looked round to see Roarke watching her, just standing in the shadows, looking. She clutched her heart. 'Oh!' It hammered with the fear of an intruder. She had not expected to see him again. 'I thought you'd gone for good,' she gasped.

He flung down several fish on to the verandah. 'I had to get away. I went fishing.' He wasn't angry any more, and that was something.

'I've been typing,' she said almost shyly. It was like talking to a stranger. 'I thought I'd do it and finish it and give it to my father for you.' She swallowed. 'I'll get you a drink.'

'No. I had one on the boat.'

'Then I'll get one for myself.' She stood up, and went inside. She had stacked all the typewritten sheets in order on the floor, underneath a large flat stone, and when she returned Roarke was looking through them.

'You've done an incredible amount,' he remarked.

'I didn't have anything else to do,' she answered simply. 'I thought I was alone again. It was the only thing.'

He replaced them and straightened up. They looked

at each other, and there was the whole world in that glance, across the shadows that surrounded them, making them both indistinct and blurred. At least, he was blurred, to her. Joanna took a deep breath. She wasn't going to cry, she *wasn't*.

'I regret my anger,' he said.

She shook her head. 'Don't. It's gone—passed.'

'No, it's not. It could happen again.'

'Yes, I suppose it could. I didn't think—we were getting on so well—it seemed——' Her voice faltered. 'It was so good——'

Then she stood tall and proud, and faced him. 'I'm sorry too,' she said. 'I was hurt and angry and I struck out—I was frightened by my anger. I——' she swayed slightly, with tiredness and unhappiness and a kind of longing to be taken care of, and protected. 'Oh, Roarke, I——'

He walked forward to her and she instinctively flinched. She could not take any more. 'Please——' she began.

He put his hands on her arms. 'I'm not going to hurt you,' he said softly. 'Don't you know? I couldn't hurt you.'

'You nearly did.' She looked up at last, at his face so close to hers. 'Please let go of my arms, please. I c-can't fight you any more, Roarke.'

'I don't want to fight you. I didn't this morning and I don't now. What I want more than anything is to make love to you—but you know that already, don't you? Dear God, it was why, when I saw you in possible danger, I really blew my top. I was terrified for you—and I was on the beach and could do nothing. If a shark had attacked you——' he swallowed. 'It would have been too late for me to save you.' His voice had gone huskier. 'That was why it turned to anger. You didn't realise—I had to go, to get out, or I don't know what I would have done.'

He had not released her. He still held her, and she felt the tears rising in her eyes, blinding her. 'Hold me,' she whispered helplessly, not knowing why she said it, and he took her to him and held her close to him, and he was trembling.

'Don't you know why I came?' he whispered softly in her ear as he stroked her hair. 'It wasn't to see Charlie, it was to see you.'

'B-but you didn't know I was here!' she said, voice muffled, pressed against his chest, a safe place to be.

'Joanna, Minnie hasn't *got* a sister in Barbados. Who do you think persuaded them to go?'

'I don't understand,' she began, and she truly didn't.

Roarke gave a sigh, drew her down on to the sand, and sat beside her, still holding her, and began to talk. Softly, insistently, he spoke, and her stunned disbelief gradually changed to a kind of wonder. It was he who had made Olivia tell her about the island, he who had planned everything like a military operation.

'When I left you with your father, I went off on a trip, as you know, and I put you out of my mind—or thought I did. You wouldn't go away. It took me nearly two months to realise what had happened to me, Joanna, and it was quite a shock. I didn't want to be in love, I didn't choose to be in love, but unfortunately for me, I was.' He tipped her chin with his finger. 'With you. So I made my plans, and I arrived "accidentally" so that you and I could have time to get to know one another better, and for me to discover if my feelings for you were in any way reciprocated.' He pulled her closer. 'Tell me if I'm the biggest fool you've ever met, and I'll accept it.'

She shook her head. 'Don't you know how I feel about you?'

'No,' he answered. 'Tell me.'

'I love you. I have almost since the beginning. Oh, Roarke, Roarke, I *love* you. I love you! I never thought I'd be able to say it——' She began to cry helplessly with sheer happiness and he caught her to him and cradled her to his chest, stroking her, soothing her.

'Oh, my darling, idiot child! You're wonderful. You're truly wonderful——' he kissed her gently, and the wonder of it all was in that kiss, a golden spiralling of excitement and tenderness and love blending.

They lay back in the darkness, holding each other tightly as if they would never let go again, and there in the grey blur of the tropical night Roarke told her of his love, and she told him of hers, then they kissed again, knowing that for both of them this was just the beginning, that there was all the time in the world, that they would never be parted again.

They slept in each other's arms, and when dawn broke they watched the sun rise together and made their plans for the future.

Roarke stroked her face as they lay beside each other. 'Dear Joanna, dearest, beloved girl,' he said softly, with the love she now knew blazing like the sun from his eyes, and his face so tender that she could not look away, nor did she want to, 'I love you more than life itself.'

'And I you,' she whispered.

'And we have a week more here together. When we leave, we'll be married.'

'Yes.'

'Wherever we go, whatever we do, we'll be together for always.'

'I know we will.' She pulled him towards her. 'Always,' she repeated softly, 'always,' and she kissed him.

# We value your opinion...

You can help us make our books even better by completing and mailing this questionnaire. Please check [✓] the appropriate boxes.

1. Compared to romance series by other publishers, do Harlequin novels have any additional features that make them more attractive?

   .1 ☐ yes          .2 ☐ no          .3 ☐ don't know

   If yes, what additional features? _____
   _____
   _____

2. How much do these additional features influence your purchasing of Harlequin novels?

   .1 ☐ a great deal  .2 ☐ somewhat  .3 ☐ not at all  .4 ☐ not sure

3. Are there any other additional features you would like to include?

   _____
   _____
   _____

4. Where did you obtain this book?

   .1 ☐ bookstore          .4 ☐ borrowed or traded
   .2 ☐ supermarket        .5 ☐ subscription
   .3 ☐ other store        .6 ☐ other (please specify)_____

5. How long have you been reading Harlequin novels?

   .1 ☐ less than 3 months   .4 ☐ 1-3 years
   .2 ☐ 3-6 months           .5 ☐ more than 3 years
   .3 ☐ 7-11 months          .6 ☐ don't remember

6. Please indicate your age group.

   .1 ☐ younger than 18   .3 ☐ 25-34      .5 ☐ 50 or older
   .2 ☐ 18-24             .4 ☐ 35-49

Please mail to: Harlequin Reader Service

In U.S.A.                    In Canada
1440 South Priest Drive      649 Ontario Street
Tempe, AZ 85281              Stratford, Ontario N5A 6W2

Thank you very much for your cooperation.